STARKAD THE VIKING

Gavin Chappell

THOR'S STONE PRESS

CONTENTS

Blessed by Odin, cursed by Thor, Starkad is doomed to wander the world for three life-spans, committing a villainous deed in each. Hated by the people, loved by murderers and tyrants, he seeks only peace, but his destiny is endless war...

The legendary warrior battles his way through three adventures:

STARKAD AND THE THUNDER GOD
STARKAD THE REBEL
STARKAD THE TRAITOR

STARKAD AND THE THUNDER GOD

1: Half Troll

ACROSS THE ICE fields strode a massive, ungainly figure.

From horizon to horizon swept the shimmering plain of ice, its monotony broken only by the blue grey hint of far-off mountains to north and south. The cold air was still and silent apart from creaks from the ice as it shifted and moved about; beneath it lay the chill waters of the river Elivagar, which resembles a vast sea of ice to all but the gods and the giants.

The man who marched across the ice had more than a drop of giant blood in his veins; he was eight feet tall, with a harsh rugged face like a troll's, but it was his many arms that revealed his otherworldly origins. Although his rough clothes, bearskin tunic and fur boots, wolfskin mantle and shark tooth necklace suggested a savage, primitive upbringing an observer might associate with the world of the giants, the four steel swords hanging from his belt indicated his familiarity with the more sophisticated lands of men.

Over his back he carried the carcass of a large white furred bear.

Thunder rumbled overhead. The giant flinched, looking up balefully. His folk had good cause to fear that din.

This was Starkad Aludreng, a renowned warrior of the Northlands, who dwelt sometimes at Alufoss in the Norse kingdom of Telemark. His mother had been a human princess, but his father Storkvid was of giant blood, and like his son had been a famous fighter both north and south of the Elivagar, that vast river that divides the world of giants from the world of men.

Starkad was heading south; the call of the world of men was strongest now. But as he lumbered across the frozen river, his grim expression, his trollish appearance, his rough attire, all combined to suggest a creature from out of a primal past. The surrounding ice field seemed his most fitting setting. He could never be truly accepted, even in those long ago days before the gods returned to earth, when trolls and monsters still shambled at the edges of that tiny circle of firelight that is human existence.

Like an exile from some savage, prehistoric age, Starkad strode the ice field undeterred.

Leagues south of there, in a rugged snowclad land closer to the world of men, Ogn Alfasprengi stood at the entrance to a cave, staring out across a chilling plain of ice and lava. With a sigh, she turned back to the dim figure that lurked in the fire lit gloom of the cave's interior.

'When did Starkad say he would return from hunting?'

Her companion shuffled into the light. While Ogn was young and beautiful, her nurse Elli was ancient, withered. Ogn's eyes were clear, shining with a youthful innocence dimmed only a little by worry, their cobalt blue enhanced by the azure snood she wore; Elli was halting, half blind. She peered up at her mistress uncertainly.

'He'll be back soon enough, I'm sure,' the nurse croaked. 'What man wouldn't return to one such as you? Besides, he is hunting the beast that your wedding guests will all dine upon.'

Ogn shrugged miserably, and glanced down at herself. Her once-beautiful green kirtle was stained and torn, her fair hair was unwashed and her body was grimy. She didn't feel beautiful.

'Oh, Elli, dear,' she said. 'I don't want to marry Starkad. He's a big brute, and much too old. I want to marry a different kind of man—handsome, dashing... young!'

'Now, we've been through this already, girl,' the old woman warned her. 'Your father wanted you to marry someone influential in the land of Jotunheim. Too long have Jotunheim and the Glittering Plains been at war, he says; we need to settle our differences and prepare for the invaders from the south...'

'But why does that mean I have to marry that evil man?' Ogn demanded, pouting. She shook her head. Politics meant little to her.

She was a maid of seventeen summers. Far too young to be marrying a man as old as Starkad. None knew his true age, but her grandfather remembered him from his youth. In the Glittering Plains the blood of men ran thick in the dwellers' veins, and many of Ogn's contemporaries were ready to make an alliance with the "invaders from the south" as Elli termed them; the Aesir and the Vanir, the warriors who had fought against Ymir the Frost-Giant in the morning of the world: cruel Thor, (said to hunt trolls and even giants for sport), cunning, perfidious Odin, lusty Frey, and all the rest.

But although the Aesir were fierce conquerors, they seemed to the younger people of the Glittering Plains better folk than the monsters who ruled Jotunheim. But the elders wanted to cling on to the old ways; though the feuds and the raids between the two countries had been present throughout their lives, they were strong believers in the old saw, "Better the troll you know." Elli was like all the rest.

'You'll marry and like it, my girl,' Elli said warningly. 'And you can put any thoughts of handsome young warriors right out of your mind.'

Ogn sighed again.

Roaring battle cries and swinging clubs, two frost giants attacked Hergrim Halftroll.

The young warrior had been wandering in Ymisland since his longship was wrecked on the shore of Gandvik, the Bay of Sorcery, killing all the crew except himself. He'd been visiting relatives in the northern reaches of Ymisland, and was sailing back to his lands in Halogaland on the edge of the world of men. But now he was lost among the mountain rocks, far from anywhere he knew, and he was continually under attack from hostile natives.

Dodging their attack, Hergrim leapt for an outcrop of rock above the giants' heads, just managing to grab hold of the ledge. He scrabbled and scuffled as he hung there, then kicked back at the wall of stone, somersaulting in the air with his sword jutting out, and came down heavily, booted feet smashing into the face of the first frost giant. The lumbering, slab-faced, heavy limbed monster went down before Hergrim's onslaught, choking and howling as the sword pierced his vitals.

The giant collapsed in bloodstained snow, a bemused expression on its heavy features, and Hergrim was flung into a nearby snowdrift. Stunned, he lay motionless for a few moments. But he soon scrambled to his feet—to find the second giant heading straight for him.

He reached for his sword, but realised it was still stuck in the other giant's guts. The surviving giant lifted his club.

Hergrim ran at him, ducking in low underneath the threatened blow. Grasping the towering figure by its ankles, he heaved... strained... and by main force lifted the giant into the air.

'Put me down!' the giant boomed, face creased with outraged bewilderment. A tiny creature like this, almost a bairn by his own titanic standards, and yet he had not only slain Geiti, he was able to lift a mighty giant like himself. These were the giant's last conscious thoughts as Hergrim, beginning to feel the strain from the heavy weight, turned and tossed him down a nearby crevasse.

As he listened in satisfaction to the giant's descent, Hergrim dusted off his hands, then went to the carcase of the first giant and yanked his sword out from its vitals. As he did so, he heard something that caused him to freeze.

'Good work, for so small a man,' croaked a voice from behind him.

Hergrim turned to see a tall but stooped figure. It was an ancient giant; male, Hergrim presumed from its looks, though the voice was weak and high-pitched. The giant wore long fur robes and held a gnarled wooden staff. A few wisps of beard grew from his chin, and two cold eyes gazed at the warrior.

'Where I come from in Eydi, I am held to be a big man,' Hergrim said. 'In the world of men, there are few who have my height.'

'But in the world of the giants, you seem like a overweening child,' the old giant quavered. 'Surely not all your ancestry is human?'

Hergrim shrugged. 'In Eydi they call me Hergrim Halftroll. My father was named Arngrim, and he raised me in the world of men, but my mother is Ama, daughter of Ymir.'

'Then we are cousins, you and I. I am Rangbeinn, Bergelmir's son. Ymir was my grandfather. It is strange that you should be younger than me, but my folk live longer than men. So what brings you to Ymisland, where our mutual ancestor once reigned—before Odin and his brothers murdered him?'

'I came to visit my kin,' said Hergrim. 'It seems I have found a long lost cousin.' He reached out and shook Rangbeinn's great paw.

'You are a mighty warrior,' Rangbeinn said, indicating the frost giants Hergrim had killed. 'Your people must be proud of you.'

Hergrim shrugged. 'I have yet to gain glory among my kind in the world of men. Folk sneer at my trollish ancestry. And yet would I win a name that will never die beneath the heavens ere I depart this life.'

Rangbeinn hummed and hawed. 'I have a notion how you might do that,' he said, 'if such a small fellow is up to the job.'

'Up to what job?' Hergrim demanded. 'You have an idea?'

Rangbeinn nodded. 'Not far from my own cavern,' he began, 'is another cave that belongs to Gudmund, king of the Glittering Plains. I have heard that his daughter Ogn Alfasprengi awaits there for her betrothed, Starkad Aludreng, who has been in Jotunheim, and means to take her to wed her in his home of Alufoss, in the world of men. Starkad...'

Hergrim paled. 'I've heard of him. He lives in the world of men, but he's more trollish than I. He has eight arms, doesn't he?'

Rangbeinn nodded. 'He's a fierce opponent, but his betrothed is one of the most beautiful maidens in the Northlands. People say she is as lovely as an elf, even the elf princess Alfhild of Alfheim! If you carry her off, and slay her trollspawned leman, you will be sure to win a name for yourself.'

Hergrim nodded. 'I'll do it,' he said quietly. 'Thanks, Rangbeinn. If there is any way I can repay you...'

'If you can kill Starkad, who has for many years terrorised much of the Glittering Plains and the borderlands, you will have repaid me indeed,' replied the old giant. 'Now I will return to my cave and prepare for the journey, to tell the king that his daughter is saved.'

Rangbeinn shuffled quietly away.

Hergrim Halftroll stared after him. On second thoughts, he wasn't at all sure about this plan. Yet it seemed the maid was not uncomely. He wrenched his sword out of the stiffening giant's breast, and strode south.

Starkad had almost reached the craggy banks of

the Elivagar by now, and his heavy heart lifted. He would soon be with his betrothed.

His rough face creased into a smile as he thought of Ogn. As fresh as snow on the wind-swept heights, as happy as a gambolling bear cub, her eyes like arctic skies, her hair like the northern lights... and she was his. Her father, Gudmund king of the Glittering Plains, had promised her to him, and they were to be married this Yule. Starkad's blood raced at the thought. What glory, to own such a maiden.

He quickened his pace, soon reaching the edge of the ice. Now he started searching for a way up the far bank. Soon he'd be at the cave where he was to meet his love.

His grim face cracked with another smile.

'Where is Starkad?' Ogn muttered. 'If I must marry him, he could at least come for me. This cave is vile.'

'This cave belongs to your father,' said her nurse. 'If you can't stand this, think what it'll be like in the world of men.'

'But I wasn't meant to live in rough conditions. Is this how he lives?'

'Nay,' said Elli, trying to hearten her. 'He has a great cavern in the world of men.'

Ogn shivered. 'The world of men,' she whispered. 'I'm frightened of humans.'

'They're naught to fear,' Elli said.

Ogn pouted. 'But you told me once that they eat giants.'

Elli smiled grimly. 'That was when you were young,' she said, 'and wouldn't go to bed when I told you.'

Ogn frowned. 'You mean they're not like that?' she demanded. 'What are they like, then?'

'Starkad has human blood, they do say,' Elli replied.

'I know enough about him to be sure that I want naught to do with his people,' Ogn replied. 'Oh, Elli, I don't have to go and live with such savages, do I?'

Before Elli could reply, Ogn heard a scuffling sound from the cave mouth. She whirled round, expecting to see her monstrous betrothed striding in to claim her. Her eyes widened. A figure loomed out of the mist.

'Are you Ogn Alfasprengi?' it asked.

Elli hobbled forward. 'Go,' she commanded forbiddingly. 'No one may see Ogn before she is married to Starkad Aludreng—certainly not a vagrant like you. Only I am allowed to tend to her needs.'

A tall, handsome man stepped into sight. Ogn gasped. Here was the man of her dreams, full of life, with a charming, affable smile, a broad, clear face, and a body that whispered of firm, powerful caresses.

'But Elli,' she cried, wonderingly. 'This is just the man I'd want as my leman.'

Elli struck her. 'Shameless hussy!' Ogn pulled away in shock, holding her stinging cheek. 'You're Starkad's, and no one else's. You'll do as your father tells you…'

'I don't think so,' the man interrupted. 'I'm here to rescue this girl from Starkad's clutches. What fool left such a beauty unguarded?'

At this, Elli turned to face him. 'Unguarded?' she hissed. 'You must first get past me.'

The man laughed. 'I'm Hergrim Halftroll,' he said. 'I've slain more giants than I can count, and a fair few men. I'm a berserk, and know all the secrets of the runes. What makes you—an old woman—think you can stop me?'

Without further ado, Elli leapt at him.

Talons burst out of the old nurse's fingertips. Her lips split open in a wolfish grin, revealing a mouth brimming with fangs. In a blur of movement, she brought her claws up, slashed back, slashed forth. Hergrim reached up to his cheek to feel a strange wetness. Lowering his hand he stared at it. It was slick with fresh blood.

He glared at the old woman, murder in his eyes. Without drawing his sword, he returned her attack.

He lunged at Elli, trying to get her in a headlock, but the old woman leapt back, hissing, spread out her claws, then came at him under his guard, slashing at his midriff. Lancing white-hot pain shot through his body, but he gritted his teeth and brought his right foot down on her instep. Elli stumbled. Hergrim grabbed her right wrist and wrenched. There was a cracking sound and Hergrim withdrew his grasp, leaving her clawed hand at an unnatural angle.

Ogn shrieked in horror. Elli tore at Hergrim with her other hand. Thinking the fight had ended, Hergrim wasn't expecting this, and he barely dodged the attack. Panting, he brought his two fists down on the nurse's head and her skull shattered, spattering him with blood and brains. Her lifeless corpse fell to the cold cave floor.

Breathing heavily, Hergrim looked up from the ghastly mess, and his eyes met those of Ogn Alfasprengi, which were wide with horror—yet tinged with a kind of admiration. 'My apologies!' He grinned, dabbing the blood off his arms with his cloak. 'I seem to have killed your nurse.'

Ogn shook her head, unable to speak. Hergrim strode across the cave floor to catch her in his arms. They embraced fiercely.

'Where is your betrothed?' he asked, taking his lips from hers. Her face paled.

'He should be here soon,' she murmured. 'We must get away. I don't want to marry an eight-armed troll.'

'Come with me, then,' Hergrim told her. 'We'll cross the border into the world of men. Stay with my father's people. Starkad will never find us there.'

Ogn bit her lip, gazing down at Elli's motionless form. Bravely, she nodded. Holding hands, they made their way outside.

Starkad Aludreng strode up the lava slope to the mouth of the cave where would meet his be-trothed. His nostrils twitched as they caught the familiar scent of freshly spilled blood.

He entered the cave, his massive heart pound-ing in his mighty chest, and his face fell as he took in the bloody scene. His eyes narrowed, and he gave a great bellow of grief. Grabbing Elli's broken corpse, he flung it against the cave wall.

Then he grew calmer. He examined the en-trance to the cave. Two pairs of footprints were visible in the cold grey sand.

'I'll get her back,' he vowed in a voice like the creaking of a glacier, 'if it's the death of me.'

2: King Of The Glit-
tering Plains

THE ICY SAND crunched beneath Starkad's great feet as he left the cave. He looked searchingly at the ground. Rocks and grit made up most of the area beyond the cave mouth, but snow and slush was visible in places. Narrowing his eyes against glare from the ice field, Starkad saw only a few footprints in the slush. It looked as if his bride's abductor had attempted to conceal any signs of their passing, but Starkad was an expert tracker. Signs that would be meaningless to most folk were entire sagas to him. He followed the trail out of the defile and down the lava slope.

Here the rock ended at the edge of the Elivagar. It was the way he had come. He had been too intent on reaching his beloved to heed any trail at the time, but now the prints leapt out at him. They led along the bank of the giant river, then up into the rocks that rose behind the cave. Here they petered out as the snow vanished, leaving only cold rocks. Here even Starkad's skill as a tracker failed him, but he could see that the trail had led in the direction of a gulch between two volcanic peaks, whose smoking cones rose high above him.

He nodded to himself. That was where they would have been heading.

He sat on a rock with the bear carcass he had been carrying over his knees and cut out its liver to eat on his journey. After wrapping this in a scrap of hide and thrusting it into his belt, he began the ascent.

From the brief signs, he pictured the interloper as a large man, almost as big as Starkad, but lighter on his feet. Younger, perhaps. Of giant blood, but no doubt it was mixed with that of the men of Midgard, like many half trolls who dwelt in these border regions. Starkad himself was the son of Storkvid the mountain giant, but his mother had been a human woman, who brought him up in the world of men, and he was equally at home with either folk—or just as much of an outcast.

Leaping from boulder to boulder, hauling himself up crags, he reached the gulch. It was empty and silent. The cold was intense, but the pumice and grit was bone dry. No snow lay anywhere. He heard a sound from above, and saw two wyverns soaring high up in the air above the tufa cliffs, their membranous wings outstretched. Starkad's great feet crunched in the cold grit as he made his way up the gulch. He paused, absently scratching his head with one of his arms. There was no sign of the half troll's hoofs or Ogn's daintier feet in the grit. Had he been led a merry chase? Had his quarry doubled back?

Starkad was about to turn round, climb back down the cliffs, and begin the search again from where the trail left off. Then he noticed a narrow cave mouth in the side of the adjacent cliff. This was an area he knew poorly, it being a possession of the giants of the Glittering Plains, the kingdom beyond Trollheim with which he and his kind had been at war for so long. Now that there was peace, now that he had been offered the maiden Ogn as part of that peace, he would learn more about the place. His schooling would begin in the newfound cave, from which he could see smoke was rising.

It had a dweller. And that dweller might have information.

Starkad found a track leading up the slope through the rocks and followed it hastily. As he did so, he heard a clatter from above, looked up, and saw a dark shape move hurriedly from the cave mouth. Grey against the grey of the rocks, it seemed to be heading away up the rock field.

It moved with haste and yet it seemed to be making poor progress. Starkad bounded over the rocks towards it. The fugitive turned towards him and Starkad saw that it was an old giant, who supported himself on a staff. The giant's face was a picture of terror. His foot slipped and he fell, cracking his head against a rock.

Starkad was at his side in seconds. The old giant had a staff in his hands and a pack on his back as if he had been setting out on a journey. But the blood that oozed from his scalp and the greyish cast of his hairy countenance showed that he was going nowhere. His breathing was shallow, hoarse. Starkad knew that he would die soon. No leech in the worlds of giants or men could save him.

Despite this, Starkad gripped him by the shoulders and shook him. 'Old fellow!' he barked. The giant's eyes flickered open and he peered vaguely at his interlocutor. 'Old fellow, why did you run?'

The giant's eyes widened. 'Starkad Aludreng! You live! The half troll...' he muttered. 'No... I must get away...'

'You'll go nowhere, old fellow,' Starkad said harshly, 'except into Hel's cold kingdom. Why did you run?' He gestured at the pack. 'You were preparing for a journey. Where would it have taken you?'

'I was going to the Glittering Plains,' the giant said painfully. 'I had a message for King Gudmund.'

Starkad grunted. 'Gudmund. A good enough fellow. I was set to marry his daughter. Some knave has reft her from me.' His eyes narrowed suspiciously. 'You dwell close to the cave where I was to meet her. The thief must have taken her from there. I found her nurse dead. Did you see aught?'

'I saw naught!' The giant's words came out in a gurgle.

'Tell the truth, old fellow,' Starkad said, 'or it'll be the worse for you!'

The old giant's laughter was a pain wracked gasp. 'What can you do to me? I'm dying, we both know that.'

'Then there is no point in dissembling,' Starkad roared. 'Where is my bride?'

'He took her,' the old giant said. 'The youngster. Hergrim Halftroll, of the blood of Arngrim the Rock Dweller. He took her so that she would not be forced to marry a monster like you. I was setting out to tell King Gudmund the good news.'

Starkad glowered down at him, shook the old giant like a dog with a rat. 'Good news? Gudmund and I worked long and hard to bring about this treaty. He would not be happy to learn that it has been spurned so! Old fellow! If you're lying...'

But the next sound from the old giant's lips was a death rattle. The trail had turned cold.

Starkad rose from the body, and stalked away. Let the old fool lie here unburied, unburnt, a prey to the wyverns that circled above the crags. Now Starkad had some notion of what had happened. Some youngster had taken his bride away.

He shook his hoary locks. He knew that he was no longer young. In his youth he had been too busy warring to find a bride. Now the war was over, he had felt joyous at the thought of settling down with a young princess of the folk he had once fought. She would be the prize of his valour, a prop for his old age, a mother for his children.

Gudmund had agreed to it after long wrangling, and threats by Starkad to bring raiders from his homeland deep into the Glittering Plains and burn the king's hall at Grund. She had been one of the terms of the treaty. Now she was taken from him. And what the old giant had said suggested that Gudmund would not be unhappy to learn of this.

He began trudging in the direction of Gudmund's kingdom.

One morning a month later, as he strode from his night's camp in the forest, he saw the land open up before him, a fair plain extending towards the rising sun. Down at the base of the crags a tributary called the Hemra ran headlong towards the greater stream of the Elivagar. Crossing it was a bridge that shone in the morning sunlight, just as the plains beyond glittered.

Through meadows and pastures he travelled, passing great herds of woolly mammoths, which were herded by Gudmund's people. Homesteads and villages became more and more frequent, many of their houses roofed with a thatch that glittered golden in the sun. At last, he reached a palisaded settlement dominated by a large gold roofed hall.

Here he addressed the giant doorkeeper. 'I am Starkad Aludreng,' he said. 'I wish to speak with King Gudmund.'

A quarter of an hour later, he stood before a dais within the gold thatched hall. Sitting on an exquisitely carved oaken chair was a tall, broad-faced, handsome man who wore ermine trimmed robes. This was Gudmund, Starkad's father in law-to-be. Ranked behind him were the giants of his hearth guard, all fully armed and clad in glittering armour. All were handsome and perfectly formed. None had more than one head, or more than two arms and legs.

'What brings Starkad Aludreng to my hall of Grund?' Gudmund boomed in a strong, resonant voice, his frank, glacier blue eyes dancing. 'I had thought that you would have taken my daughter south to your home at Alufoss!' His eyes narrowed. 'Where is Ogn?'

'It is for that reason that I come here, O king,' Starkad rumbled. 'I returned from my hunting over the Elivagar only to find Ogn's nurse brutally slain—and my prospective wife missing!'

A cry of horror came from the assembled giants.

'Aye,' said Starkad, 'and when I tried to hunt down her abductor I lost them among the rocks. But I have learnt the name of the princess's abductor.'

'Who is this caitiff?' boomed Gudmund, sitting up in his chair. 'Lead me to him, and I will carve his heart out!'

'I do not know where he is,' said Starkad, 'but his name at least I know. He is Hergrim Halftroll of the blood of Arngrim the Rock Dweller. I come seeking news of this halftroll.'

'His name is not sung widely,' said Gudmund, 'but I know of his kin. I have heard of his father —a vicious robber on the margins of the world of men. He carried off Ama Ymir's-Daughter in early days.' The giant king ground his teeth, then slammed a ham-like hand against a broad palm. 'I shall send out my spies and my hawks, and we will learn where he has gone. And when we do, you and I, Starkad Aludreng, shall hunt him down and kill him.'

◆ ◆ ◆

'Well, what news?'

Starkad's voice rang harshly through the hall as a messenger strode in, having dismounted his mammoth in the yard outside. A slender giant with a bald head, he looked to King Gudmund.

The king waved his hand. 'First have yourself a stoop of ale to wash the dust from your throat,' he offered, and a giantess hurried towards the messenger with a brimming horn.

Starkad knocked the horn from the giantess' hand with such force she herself went sprawling. The horn clattered down beside the dais, spilling its contents to the rush strewn floor. 'Enough of this!' Starkad shouted. He whirled round to the startled messenger. 'I called for news! Months have passed with no word!'

The messenger gave him a dark look. 'No news yet,' he replied, and went to help the giantess to her feet. 'We think they have travelled far south into the world of men.'

'Sit down,' said Gudmund commandingly to Starkad. 'You are making a spectacle of yourself. It's that fire giant blood.'

Starkad glowered. 'There is no fire giant blood

in my veins!' But he sat, and tried to solace himself with the thought that half of Gudmund's household troop was out searching for the errant princess and her halftroll abductor.

'Surely you're concerned about what this vagrant might be doing with your daughter?' he barked at Gudmund.

The king of the Glittering Plains inclined his head. 'I am,' he said in sorrow, 'but I know that naught will be achieved by precipitate action. That said, for all we know, Hergrim Halftroll could be treating her with the utmost courtesy.'

Starkad stared at him wordlessly.

'Bad taste, I realise,' said Gudmund. 'An obscure warrior who spends much of his time in the worlds of men takes my daughter by violence...' He shook his head. 'What father would not be angry? But until messengers return with news of her, we must remain calm.'

He clicked his fingers at the giantess who by now had recovered. 'Bring ale, for our brave messenger and for my guest. No, not ale—wine. Wine of the Southlands. We shall have a carouse tonight that will rid your mind of these thoughts.'

'How can I carouse when Ogn is in that hands of that murderer?' Starkad grumbled. But he accepted a jewelled goblet from the servant and moodily drank the blood red liquid.

The following month more messengers came, and this time they brought good news.

'I spoke with the beasts of the earth and the

birds of the air,' said the forest giant, reporting to Gudmund, 'and to the little people who labour at their forges beneath the earth. It was one of these dwarfs who told me that he had word of a halftroll and a giant maiden who had set up a homestead at Eydi in Midgard. The beauty of the maiden has spread far and wide through the forest, almost as beautiful as Princess Alfhild of Alfheim, rumour said, and the dwarfs nurtured lecherous thoughts within their caves. I say maiden...' The forest giant paused, and a mournful expression crossed his brown, pitted face.

Gudmund leaned forward in his seat, face urgent. 'Go on.'

'Yes, go on!' Starkad barked.

The forest giant looked from one to the other. 'The dwarf told me that he had heard that the belly of this girl was big with child.'

'Bergelmir's Ark!' Starkad swore violently. He swung round to Gudmund. 'You hear that? He has raped her! We must set out at once to regain her and wreak vengeance!'

He rose and shouted, 'Guards! Warriors! To arms! Bring me a mammoth! We ride to Midgard!'

'Sit!' said Gudmund commandingly. The king of the Glittering Plains looked upon Starkad. 'Would you presume to issue orders under my own roof?'

Starkad subsided and sat down. Even as he did so, there was a rush of footsteps from the doors and guards hurried in.

'Sire?' said the captain of the guard, a bearlike

giant with a great blonde beard. 'Should I give the sign for a general muster? Send out the war arrow? What is happening?'

'We have found where my daughter is living,' said Gudmund. 'It seems that she is now a mother to be.'

'We must rescue her,' said Starkad.

Gudmund gave it some thought. 'I shall send you on this mission,' he told Starkad. 'Accompanied by a small force of my giants, you shall ride to Eydi and slay my daughter's ravisher. I would suggest you slay her too.'

Starkad glared at him. 'What is this foolery?' he barked.

Gudmund was cold. 'She is no daughter of mine,' he said, 'now she has parted her thighs for a half troll. If you want her, she is yours, but all will know that your woman's first child was a bastard, and not your own. If you want this stain on your honour...'

Starkad stared at him in shock. He rose again. 'Bring me my swords and a mammoth to ride,' he bellowed. 'I shall go alone if need be!'

'You'll require my men to guide you,' said Gudmund, looking up from a whispered conversation with the captain of the guard. 'Lopti will lead them.'

The captain clicked his mighty fingers at several of his warriors, and followed Starkad from the hall.

Dawn of the next day found them riding

on mammoth-back across the Glittering Plains. Starkad rode in a gloomy silence, while the giants of Gudmund's guard chattered amongst themselves.

Starkad had no need for an escort. He knew the location of Eydi, having dwelt a long time at Alufoss, not many leagues away, and he would travel faster without Gudmund's aid. The giant king's attitude seemed strange to him. Now that Ogn was no longer a maid, he was willing to cast her aside. Starkad was not so callous. He would fight for Ogn, make the beautiful giant maiden his own. The bastard, if it were born, could be left to die on the mountainside, and then Starkad would father his own son.

They crossed the Hemra by the golden bridge, Starkad still in the lead. As Lopti and the rest rode down behind him, the captain declared:

'We're no longer on our king's lands. What we do now is no breach of hospitality.'

Perplexed, Starkad turned. Lopti lifted a javelin from his saddle and flung it. Growling, Starkad snatched the weapon from the air with a hand and reversed it. The giants fanned out, trying to encircle him, each of them holding javelins.

'What treachery is this?'

Lopti sneered. 'You were a fool to come unaccompanied to the Glittering Plains, trollspawn,' he said. 'Know you not that all loathe you here? We have not forgotten your depredations. My king was playing a long game when he agreed to let his daughter wed you.'

Starkad snarled. 'The half troll! Gudmund was in this with him?'

Lopti shook his head. 'The half troll had naught to do with it. We know naught of him. Gudmund conceded to your demands when you rode to his hall bringing a threat of raiders. Now you have come as a suppliant, a weakling who begs for aid. He has disowned his daughter; and it was through your fault that she was exposed to the risk of rape. He no longer owes any obligation towards you, except that of vengeance!' Lopti raised his sword. 'Kill him!'

Before the giants could respond, Starkad flung the javelin. It impaled Lopti, knocking him rolling over the back of his mount.

Sawing at the reins of his mammoth, Starkad rode off in a hailstorm of javelins. As two missiles sank into the hairy hide of his mount on either side of him, he vanished into the forest.

The giants pursued him for a while, but soon he had lost them among the trees.

His mammoth died of its wounds a week later, after a long and weary journey south into the world of men. Without a mount, Starkad travelled on foot, his great strides eating up the leagues. But the world of men was a big place, and although he knew where Eydi was to be found, he also knew that he had a long journey ahead of him.

3: The Duel At Efsta Foss

'IT'S A BOY,' said Ogn, smiling tiredly.

Hergrim held up the new-born to the sun of noon that shone down on the meadow. Ogn sat in the porch of the turf roofed longhouse her man had built with his own large, capable hand, gazing up at him. The red little squalling thing gave vent to a yell.

'Oh, hand it here,' she said indulgently. 'Poor thing's hungry.'

Hergrim didn't reply, staring in wonder at this, the greatest work of his own hands. Going to the edge of the pool, he scooped up a cupped palmful of water and dashed it on his baby's head.

'I name you Grim,' he said in a low voice.

Ogn came over to join them. Plucking Grim from Hergrim's hands she set him to her pap. The precious little creature instinctively put his lips to her engorged nipple and sucked hungrily. Hergrim watched in contentment.

Hearing a rustle from the trees on the far side of the meadow, Hergrim turned.

Eyes wide, gazing at the tall, malformed figure now climbing over the forest fence, he reached out and shook Ogn's shoulder.

'Ogn,' he whispered. 'Ogn!'

'What is it, my love?'

When Ogn looked up from cooing at little Grim, her face paled and she almost dropped her baby in her shock. As the newcomer stalked down the meadow towards them, she wrapped her arms protectively round Grim and the baby broke out into lusty cries.

'Get back inside,' said Hergrim. 'Hide the baby and bring me my longsword.'

Ogn took off, her bare legs white in the sunlight as she ran for home, clutching Grim to her pap. Hergrim strode forwards to intercept their visitor. He saw that hoary old head and those eight arms, and though he had never seen him before, he recognised Starkad Aludreng.

'What brings such a troll to my lands?' he said, hand on the haft of his axe. 'Be off with you. This is the world of men, not Trollheim.'

'I am of the blood of the mountain giants,' Starkad said. 'It is you who are half a troll. And I am an honourable warrior, not a ravisher of women.'

'I ravished no woman,' Hergrim told him. 'Ogn came with me willingly.'

Starkad shook his hoary locks. 'Promised me by her father, the king of the Glittering Plains, she was. You seduced her and stole her from me.'

Hergrim wasn't much shorter than this mountain giant, though he had only two arms. If only Ogn would be quicker getting him his sword. Starkad had four swords hanging from his belt;

right now all Hergrim had to defend himself was an axe, once a weapon of war but now much blunted after being pressed into service for tree felling.

'To the strong belong all things,' he said.

'Then Ogn is mine.' Starkad drew all four swords at once with a metallic ring that was sharply audible over the roar of the nearby falls. Hergrim bundled his cloak over his left arm, brandished his axe, and came to meet him in the middle of the meadow.

With his axe, he parried one sword cut, deflected another with his cloak, dodged back to avoid a cut from a third direction, but as he did so he felt a cold slash of fire across the ribs near his heart when Starkad's fourth sword fleshed him. He jumped back a few paces, then circled the huge warrior in a half crouch.

'You're at an advantage over me,' he told the giant, grinning. 'Throw away a few of those swords and meet me like a man, not a troll.'

'It is you who is the troll,' Starkad repeated. 'The giants of the Glittering Plains often taunted me for my freakishness, but my arms stood me in good stead in war against them. I shall cast away neither my swords nor my advantage. Instead, I shall kill you.'

He crossed the turf in a single bound, swinging all four swords at once. Hergrim retaliated in a flurry of movement, twisting and turning to parry each attack one by one. The clash of blade on blade rang out across the meadow, resounding from the timbers of the forest.

Hergrim panted. Sweat ran down his back. The monster he was fighting showed no sign of exertion. Up until now, Hergrim had been fighting on the defensive; partly because he was guarding his land, partly because he had had no opportunity to do more than parry his assailant's multiple blows. Starkad paused, opened his mouth to bellow more abuse, and it was then that Hergrim struck, hacking at the giant's unprotected midriff.

But the blade made no impression, almost as if Starkad was immune to weapons. When the giant brandished all four blades to bring them down on him, Hergrim remembered the spell his father had taught him. Despite his uncanny heritage, he was not one to rely overmuch on trollcraft and sorcery, yet this charm could be what he needed in this situation. Rather than lift his axe in vain attempt to block all four blows, as the swords descended he muttered the words of the spell.

On returning to the longhouse, Ogn laid little Grim down in his cradle beside the hearth. The chime of blade on blade drifted in through the shuttered window. She searched desperately in a chest for Hergrim's sword. He had put it away months ago, saying he no longer had any use for it, although he still wore his axe, mainly used for tree felling now and hacking back brambles ... Where, oh, where had he put it?

Grim began crying again. Torn between one responsibility and another, Ogn felt like tearing out her long fair locks. She ran over to the cradle, picked up Grim, pulled down her kirtle and set him to sucking at her pap. Still holding him she hurried back to the chest and one-handed continued to root through it as the sound of fighting continued from the meadow.

The sword was not in the chest. Where could it be? Where had he put it? She remembered clearly the day he had said he would give up his warring ways to stay with her and the then unborn child. He remembered him saying he would put the sword away... where? Of course!

In the loft! Hergrim had said he would leave the sword in the loft! She ran over to the ladder, still carrying Grim at her breast, then one handed, she climbed, shushing at her babe who chose that moment to let go and bawl loudly. She hated to think what would happen to the child if Starkad got past Hergrim and into the longhouse.

At the top of the ladder, she peered round in the gloom, absently rocking and shushing the baby. The clatter of steel on steel was still distantly audible. Where was that sword?

Ravens circled overhead, attracted by the hope of

carrion. Hergrim dodged to one side and his eyes blazed as the sword swung towards him. It struck him a glancing blow, almost heavy enough to break bones, but now it was blunt, as if the smith had forgotten to give it an edge.

'What witchery is this?' Starkad roared. He flung the sword away and it slithered down the grassy slope.

'You call me a half troll,' Hergrim replied. 'Well, my father taught me some trollcraft, at least.' His gaze was scorching. 'Attack me with four swords, and I'll blunt the edge of each!'

Now Starkad only bore three swords in his many hands. Listening to Hergrim's words, he nodded darkly. 'I've heard of he-witches like you,' he said. 'My own hide is tough enough, but that's my giant nature, not filthy sorcery...'

He struck, swinging another sword. Hergrim leapt back and fixed his eyes on the blade. The edge tarnished and went blunt even as he stared at it.

'I'm evening up the odds,' said Hergrim, 'since you won't play fair. You have your trollish eight arms, I have my father's magic to give me an edge —and to take yours!'

Starkad thrust his two remaining blades behind his back, out of sight of Hergrim, like a child with something to hide. With a free hand, he beckoned his opponent onwards.

There it was! Glimmering in the gloom, hanging from the loft pillar by a sword belt, still sheathed; Hergrim's sword. Hushing the babe now at her hip, Ogn reached out to lift it down one-handed. It was heavy! She almost overbalanced trying to get it down. Grim wailed.

'Shush! Hush, little baby!' she cooed, but to no avail. She cursed under her breath, left the sword dangling, and climbed back down the ladder, Grim at her pap. From outside she heard again the sound of fighting. Her man still resisted the interloper.

She laid Grim down in the cradle as gently but as fast as she could. From the meadow, she heard Hergrim shout, 'Ogn! Where are you! My sword! Ogn!'

As Grim burst into more wailing, she raced over to the ladder again and scurried up to the loft. This time she could reach it with more ease, though it still weighed down her slim arms. She thudded to the edge of the loft and lowered the sword down by the belt, letting it drop among the rushes on the floor. Still Grim bawled, still the noise of fighting filtered in through the unshuttered window. She jumped down the ladder, snatched up the sword, dithered by Grim's cradle, then rushed out into the meadow.

Starkad only carried two swords now, both of which for some reason he held behind his back. As Ogn came out of the door, carrying Hergrim's longsword, Hergrim hacked a blow at him with his axe. Starkad swung at him with one sword. Ogn saw Hergrim's eyes blaze as he glared at the blade, which Starkad dropped at once, but even as he did, even as Hergrim's eyes raged, the giant brought the other sword round from the far side, and sank it deep into Hergrim's heart.

Ogn's screams mingled with the bawling from the cradle.

As the half troll's body fell with a thump to the turf, Starkad whirled round. He saw the source of the screaming; a female figure in the porch of the homestead. With a shock, he recognised his be-trothed. It had been so long since he had last seen her. What was she yelling at?

'Stop your noise, girl,' he shouted over the roar of the falls her. 'Haven't I killed your ravisher? Avenged your shame?'

Ogn's face was white. Even as Starkad approached, she stripped the scabbard from the sword, placed its hilt on the earth, and flung herself upon it.

The blade slid through her breast as if through butter, jutting out of her back for a whole foot. Blood slicked the point. Blood dripped from the engorged nipple of her bare pap like crimson milk. Blood pooled on the earth beneath her.

By the time Starkad reached her, Ogn's life was ebbing fast.

'Foolish girl!' he cried in despair. 'Why have you done this?'

She looked painfully up at him, and gave him a mocking smile.

'You killed the man I loved,' she gasped. 'I won't outlive him. In there is our child. Grim's his name. You can...'

Blood gushed from her mouth, and her head slumped forward.

Starkad stared in silence at her lifeless body, while the cries and howls from inside the longhouse grew weaker and weaker. At last, he lifted his shaggy head, puzzled, and stepped inside the longhouse.

The cries emanated from a small cradle beside the fire. He crossed to it in a stride, and stood staring down at the tiny scrap of life that lay there scowling at him, red-faced and angry. Stooping, Starkad reached out a hand, and one tiny arm sprang up to seize his forefinger in a tight grasp.

Starkad nodded approvingly. 'Grim,' he said, 'you have the fire and the strength of your mother. And your father was a worthy opponent, who I slew with difficulty.'

Disengaging his finger gently, he looked around the homestead, imagining it when Ogn and Hergrim had dwelt here, full of life and happiness. All that remained of their happiness was the tiny babe, who was now bawling again.

Starkad picked him up. He would fling Grim at the wall, end his life. It would be a deed of mercy.

Then he shook his head.

'I will take you with me, youngling,' he said. 'My

wandering days are done. It is high time I settled down. I shall rear you as my own.'

He turned and strode from the longhouse.

A week later, Starkad was coming down a valley in Telemark, a place he knew well, with the baby sitting on his shoulder. On the far side of the valley was another waterfall; not the one he remembered as the place where his love died, but Alufoss, where he had his home.

Caring for the baby had been an unexpected responsibility, but for much of the journey he had employed a beggar-woman he met on the road. Having just lost a baby herself, she haf made a fine wet nurse. Now she had gone on her road, after being handsomely paid by Starkad with booty plundered from far-off lands, while the giant himself was going home.

He strode into the village at twilight. People came out to meet him, alerted by a lookout in a tower at the edge of the valley. Starkad had been gone many months, and the valley folk all hurried to welcome their champion.

'But where is the bride you went to wed, Aludreng?' asked Snjalli, the biggest farmer in these parts, a tall, skinny fellow. 'I see you bring a babe.' His face fell. 'Did she die in childbirth?'

His wife came forward, cooing, and took Grim from Starkad's shoulder. As she cradled the babe in her arms, she murmured, not looking up, 'Did your mama go to another place, then? Did she go to the land beyond the sunset?' Grim bawled, and his little hands went questing for her dry pap. 'We'll need someone to nurse him,' she added briskly, still not looking up. One of the thralls brought a pitcher of milk and she wet a cloth and let Grim suck on it.

Starkad said naught. Snjalli clapped him on the arm. 'He's a fine lad, Aludreng. You must be proud of yourself. He'll carry on your family line.'

Starkad looked at him balefully, and Snjalli quailed. 'That he will not,' the warrior said. 'He's not my boy.' The giant explained what had happened. 'Under the circumstances, I resolved to would foster him.'

'Isn't your foster dada good to you?' Snjalli's wife said. Grim burped loudly.

Snjalli was less impressed. 'You'd foster your enemy's bastard?' he asked. Starkad glowered at him again. 'Forgive me, Aludreng, but from what you say your foe carried off your bride and raped her, fathering this ravisher's get on her. Now you intend to raise it as your foster child. What will people say? That our mighty lord, the giant Starkad Aludreng, is losing his wits, that he no longer stands up for himself.

'When you were away, no raiders would come near, because they knew you were our lord, they knew that if they attacked us, you would track them down and slaughter them. But now? If they think you won't stand up for yourself, they'll think you won't stand up for your people.'

Starkad snatched the baby, grabbed the milk, and stomped off up the hill path towards the falls where he had his cavern. Grim wailed. Snjalli called after Starkad, 'There will be raiders, Aludreng, mark my words! Down from the hills or up from the sea, raiders will come if they think you can no longer guard your people.'

Starkad halted at the top of a rise, in the shadow of a pine. 'Get the lad a wet nurse, Snjalli, and cease your blather. I will guard this valley, don't fret like an old woman. But I will raise this boy as my own and I'm hearing no arguments.' He stomped away.

Following the path along the stream led him to the Alufoss, a roaring waterfall much larger than that where Hergrim Halftroll had established his own homestead. Here was Starkad's dwelling, a cavern accessed by a path under the waterfall. Hefting Grim on his shoulder, Starkad strode up to the sheet of water, noting the way the baby gurgled in contentment on hearing the sound of the falls.

Passing under the spray, Starkad entered his cavern, finding it cold, stale and dank. No homecoming for a hero, but was Starkad a hero anymore? Snjalli didn't seem to think so.

Starkad laid the boy down in a basket he intended to use as a cradle and went back out to get firewood.

News spread about the countryside: the giant of Alufoss had fallen into his dotage, that he could no longer guard the folk of his valley. Only a week later, houses on the edge of the valley were attacked in the night and several sheep and goats were driven off. Snjalli mustered an expedition to go after the raiders, but they had little success, returning after losing three men to an ambush, and regaining none of the stolen livestock.

Starkad only learnt of the attack the following morning, when Snjalli's men returned, carrying their dead and wounded on their shields. Starkad left his foster son in the care of the Lappish wet nurse Snjalli's wife had chosen from the thrall women, sharpened the swords that Hergrim Halftroll had blunted, and stomped off into the hills alone, on the trail of the raiders. After a brief fight with four or five ill equipped men he herded homewards the stolen flock, returning the following evening.

As he reached the ridge from which he could first see the pine swathed slopes and the silver thread of the falls, he halted in dismay. Smoke belched up into the sky from several places, not the smoke of cooking fires but of burning houses. In the distance, he saw longships sailing speedily away from the shore.

Cursing, terrified despite himself that little

Grim was dead or enslaved, he went bounding down the mountainside, driving the bleating sheep helter skelter before him, to see how the valley folk had fared.

Grim-faced, Snjalli and several of his kin met Starkad in the meadow in the middle of the valley. 'This happened because you abandoned us in our hour of need, Aludreng!' Snjalli said, glaring up at Starkad.

'What of Grim?' Starkad demanded. 'What of my fosterling?'

'The vikings didn't get as far up the valley as Alufoss,' Snjalli's wife reassured him. 'You're safe up there. It was the fishermen who bore the main brunt.'

Starkad relaxed. He turned to Snjalli, gesturing at the flocks he had been herding. 'I was away tracking down the last raiders,' he said. 'I brought back the sheep they stole. I did not abandon you.'

'The raiders come,' Snjalli said, 'because they hear that you are no longer man enough to lead our defences.'

'And how did they hear that?' Starkad said. 'Who put that lying yarn about?' He banged his breastbone. 'I am no weakling, even if I am foster father to my dead enemy's child. Grim means more to me than your petty insults, Snjalli. But mark my words, I will defend this valley, whatever it takes.'

Leaving the flock for its owners to claim, he turned and plodded up the valley towards Alufoss.

4: *Starkad's Despair*

S TARKAD GAZED AT the wet nurse as she let Grim suck, Ogn on his mind as he tried to think of a way to prove himself in the eyes of the world—of the worlds. They had to know that he was a strong man, that he would guard his own. What could he do? If only he had a helpmeet with him, someone like Ogn at his side, she would be able to counsel him.

One night he asked the wet nurse, but she shook her head.

'Why you want to prove yourself?' she asked. He explained as simply as he could. Her inscrutable Lappish face pondered the dilemma. 'You lost girl, girl second beautifulest in all worlds?' Starkad nodded impatiently. 'Why you content with her?'

'What?' Starkad barked. Grim began to cry.

Once the wet nurse had quieted him she looked up again. 'Why not make beautifulest girl in all worlds wife? Then all respect you.'

'Princess Alfhild...?' Starkad gazed off into the distance, excited yet appalled by the idea. 'Make the princess of the elves my wife? King Alf won't like that! It will be spoken of in all the worlds there are.' He was startled by the wet nurse's cunning. 'Raiders would surely leave the valley alone if they heard about this...! Grim would grow up in a settled land. And it would shut Snjalli's snout.'

'King wouldn't like?' the wet nurse asked.

Starkad glanced at her. Maybe she wasn't so clever after all. 'He won't give her to me gladly,' he explained. 'Besides, I won't make a new name for myself by meekly asking him for his daughter's hand in marriage. He's been saving her up for someone important. Someone big.'

There was a rumble of thunder from outside. Starkad looked upwards uneasily, seeing the cave roof, but his mind travelling out into the autumn sky. 'If the worlds are to learn that my people are well defended, I must make a show of force. I shall journey to the world of the elves and carry off the princess.'

'Carry off?' the wet nurse asked. 'Like Hergrim Halftroll? If she betrothed to man, he be angry?'

Starkad shrugged. 'Angry? He'll be furious if he's any kind of man. But that doesn't matter. What matters is my name, my reputation. That's what will ensure peace in this land. War with others!'

'What if betrothed comes for revenge?' the wet nurse asked.

'Then I'll kill him,' said Starkad simply.

Again, thunder rumbled, somewhere out to sea.

The wet nurse's idea gave Starkad new hope. The

rest of that month he spent preparing for an autumnal raid of the world of the elves. He would go alone, since that would gain him greater glory, rather than raising a crew from Snjalli's kin. For that he would need a boat small enough to require only a one man crew but large enough to survive the journey through the seas of darkness required to take him to the elf world. He would also need a good idea of the ground he would have to cover on reaching it.

He had never been to Alfheim, but he knew that much of it was wooded. Alf was its king, and he dwelt at Gimle in the midst of the forest, a bright city of graceful towers and bridges amid the trees. The world was the property of the god Frey, who had been given it as a tooth gift when young. Yet Starkad had no fear of that peaceful deity. Frey was no warrior, but a leman of peace and prosperity.

Starkad went down to his boatsheds and inspected the vessels there. They had been there since his father's day; some of their timbers were rotten and needed replacing. He had not sailed out on raiding expeditions for a few years, not since coming to terms with the king of the Glittering Plains. Well, that was all in the past now.

With the aid of some fishermen, he prepared a small vessel for the expedition into Alfheim, replacing rotten or broken strakes, renewing the rigging and prevailing upon the fishermen's wives to re-stitch the sail. On the second day of work Snjalli came down to see what was happening.

'You mean to go out in that?' he asked, openly insolent. 'In the summer my men and I went raiding in a longship. We brought back much booty after raiding ships and islands and villages. What do you hope to achieve?'

Starkad restrained a desire to seize his neighbour and fling him into the chilly waters of the fjord. 'I am going on an expedition, Master Snjalli,' he said through gritted teeth. 'I am not going to fight Vikings.'

Snjalli's lip curled. 'You hope to go fishing?' he said, as if fishing was some shameful, unmanly deed. The men helping Starkad replace the rigging paused to glower at him.

'I hope to go fishing,' Starkad said, 'for the biggest fish in these or any other waters.'

Snjalli's jaw flapped open. 'You mean to go hunting for the Midgard Serpent?' He jumped at an explanation. 'Even Thor had no success in that expedition. What madness has seized you now?'

'I do not go fishing for Jormungand,' Starkad said, returning to his work as if Snjalli was not there. 'I have bigger fish than that to fry.'

Snjalli wandered off wearing a puzzled expression.

Starkad paid the fishermen with gold rings from his hoard and they returned to their work. He noticed Snjalli watching from the entrance to his longhouse up the valley, and spent the rest of the day engaged in minor tasks round the boatsheds as the fully rigged boat rode at anchor in the road-stead off shore.

He returned to his longhouse as the sun set, gracing the headland at the edge of the fjord with a rosy glow. For a moment, it seemed to Starkad that the promontory had been drenched in blood.

He rose around midnight. The wet nurse knew the plan, although no one else did, unless she had blabbed to Snjalli's folk. The autumn night was not too cold, though a wind stirred, coming in off the sea. As Starkad made his way down the valley, his great feet thudding on the turf. The cold night sky above was spangled with stars. He thought he heard another rumble of thunder.

Reaching the boatsheds, he waded out to where his boat lay at anchor. As he hauled himself aboard, the boat almost capsized under his sudden weight before bobbing back up again. He unreefed the sails, and raised the anchor. The breeze filled his sail. Slowly he drifted out into the open waters of the fjord, and he began sailing towards the fjord entrance. It was a long voyage to the world of the elves, and Starkad had told the wet nurse that it was unlikely that he would be back before the end of autumn.

At first, Starkad sailed through seas traversed by men, passing longships and curraughs, galleys and dromonds. But soon he found himself entering unknown seas, seas where the stars were strange, where the sun never rose. He sailed for longer than he could tell through pitch blackness, where even sunstones or compasses were useless. He was sailing into the west, or so he hoped. Westward was the way to Alfheim, to the world of the elves; so tradition had it. And now tradition was his only navigator.

After almost tearing out the bottom of his boat on unseen reefs, he began to despair of ever reaching his destination. It had been a crazy idea. Sailing to the world of the giants had been different, it was a place he knew well, over the Elivagar in lands where his father had dwelt long ago. But the world of the elves was another world entirely, the place of hidden folk. Some said it lay westward, others maintained it was under the ground, with dwarfs and the dead. But surely it was the swart elves who lived in such gloomy conditions, Starkad thought, gazing round at the sightless night surrounding his ship. King Alf's folk were the elves of light, second only in power to the Aesir themselves, Odin's people.

Now Starkad saw on the horizon a green grey line, above which flew dark dots that must be birds. The dark seas opened out like a window on seas of light in a summer sunshine that poured its light down from beyond the clouds. Starkad had not dreamed that the dark seas he had traversed might conceal such beauty. Now the ruby glow seemed redundant as yellow light poured down from the welkin. He had passed out of darkness into seas of light. Looking back he could see the line of darkness behind him, from which he had come.

Seeing an inlet some way ahead, he crossed to the steering oar and guided his vessel towards the bay. Shortly afterwards he had moored the boat in a little sandy cove, overhung with trees and bushes. The scent of rotting leaves was almost overpowering. The sun glimmered down through the russet leaved trees and the air was chill. Starkad stepped ashore, hands resting on the pommels of his swords as he examined his new surroundings.

A winding path led up the bank and into the trees. Nobody was around. It seemed that he had entered the world of the elves without being seen, despite the eerie nature of his arrival.

He strode up the path. The trees leaned over his path, roofing it like a red brown tunnel. Birds sang upon the boughs, and the undergrowth was alive with the scurrying of small animals. The path grew steeper as he ascended the side of a plateau then it levelled out again. At times, through gaps in the foliage, he caught glimpses of distant mountains.

Reached the head of a valley, he gazed down at what seemed to be a city. Gimle, he supposed. Delicate towers of white and cream rose among the trees, while walkways led from bough to bough. Treehouses occupied many of the trees. A stream ran through the middle of the valley, crossed by a wooden bridge. Outside the city meadows ran down to the banks of the stream. To one side of the main gate was a grove of trees, in the centre of which was a megalithic altar.

Elves were to be seen throughout the city, some working at handicrafts, others patrolling the walkways. Still more were visible riding through the meadows. Starkad remained where he was, watching and waiting. The city seemed a haven of tranquillity. He remembered the cold home of the giants, and the savage world of men. Alfheim was apparently a peaceful and prosperous place. And yet those guards looked as if they could handle themselves in a fight.

As Starkad watched, he saw a group of elf maidens depart from the main city gate, accompanied by a few elf men in armour. Reaching the meadows, they danced in rings, holding hands, carousing and revelling as several elfin minstrels played from a recumbent stone on the meadow's edge. Amidst them danced one elf maiden who was more beautiful than the rest. Even at this distance, Starkad was certain he had found Princess Alfhild.

He made his way down the slope, lumbering from tree to tree. He didn't want any of the elves to see him. They would know that the presence of an interloper from another world did not bode well. At last he reached the valley floor. Willows grew along the stream and he concealed himself among them as he approached the meadows where Princess Alfhild and her maidens played.

At last he reached the edge of the meadows.

As he hid behind a withered trunk, he heard clear, bright voices drifting across the leaf strewn sward, mingled with the strains of the fiddles.

'It is time for the feast, fair maidens,' trilled Princess Alfhild. 'While my father makes his offering in the ring of stones, deep in the forest, we will have our own autumn feast!' The other elves gathered around her. Handmaidens spread sheets on the grass on which everyone sat cross-legged, and food was laid out for them all to eat, cold meats and salads. Bottles of wine and mead were uncorked and soon full goblets sparkled in the elf maidens' hands. Laughter rang out across the meadow.

Starkad watched the male elves, who stood talking quietly in a small group to one side. As guards they seemed negligent, and laughed and joked with the maidens and the minstrels rather than keeping an eye on their surroundings. Starkad gripped his swords and readied himself. His eyes fixed on Princess Alfhild. The rumours of her beauty had not been exaggerated, he told himself. She was indeed even more beautiful than Ogn Alfasprengi.

Tall for a woman, and slender, she had fair hair that swept down her back, while her green gown was spun from silk. Round her throat blazed jewels of the whiteness of diamonds, but they were not as comely as her face. And her only guards were four or five elf warriors, who seemed to have no thought in their heads but of dallying with white throated maidens. Starkad's lip curled.

He awaited his moment. Now the warriors were drinking, having been handed goblets by hand-maidens who had come tripping up to them, eyes wide and admiring. This would be too easy.

He burst out from the willows, swords flashing in the spring sunlight, ran straight through a group of dancing maidens and decapitated the first of the guards with a single swing of a sword. Screams and shrieks erupted from slender throats as the head, clasped in an exquisitely wrought winged helmet, landed with a splash in a fruit sorbet. Blood fountained from the headless torso, which took a step forward then toppled backwards into the nearest elf guard, who turned, looking pale, and menaced Starkad with a halberd. Starkad sneered as the guards hurried to stop him, spun round, whirling his swords, and sent them falling on every side, spattering the sweet meadow with their blood.

The slaughter took seconds. Elf maidens and minstrels ran shrieking for the city. Starkad pur-sued them, cutting down two fleeing minstrels. The princess stood proudly in the centre of the meadow as her handmaidens urged her to run.

'Who are you?' she demanded, her voice vibrant with hauteur. She was magnificent as she walked fearlessly towards him. 'Begone from this place, troll!'

'My name is Starkad!' he bellowed, running to-wards her. 'Starkad Aludreng! Hear that name, elves of Alfheim! Remember it!'

He seized her and despite her struggles, slung her over his shoulder. Her handmaidens tried to grab her from him but he knocked them aside with blows. He bent down to snatch up a few stray goblets—pure gold they were, as far as he could tell—and thrust them into his waist belt, then turned, hitched the angry princess to a more convenient position on his shoulder, and ran for the side of the valley.

Horns were belling out from the city now as the maidens streamed in with their tale of woe, but Starkad thought he could make it into the thick forest before the full guard was mustered or before the king came to rescue his daughter. Although she struggled and spat like a wildcat, he noticed that her flesh against his shoulder was warm and soft, and she exuded a delicate scent like a rose in summer.

As he ran past the willows, she shouted to him, 'Put me down! Put me down—what is your name, trollspawn? Starkad? Put me down, Starkad! What is the meaning of this?'

'You,' he panted, still running, 'are to be my bride.'

She began struggling again. When she realised that this was futile, clamped as she was in the iron grasp of his arms, she went limp. 'Nay,' she cried. 'I will not be your wife! I am Princess Alfhild of Alfheim. Even Thor of the Aesir praises my beauty. Sif herself is said to be jealous of me. I will not become the wife of an ugly, deformed troll.' She was furious.

Starkad laughed. 'Savage little kitten,' he taunted her. 'Look back at your city, princess, because it's the last time you'll see it. You're mine. You will bear fine sturdy sons for me, a line that will be conquerors, which will gain an ever living name.'

'You've carried me off,' she wailed, 'just to glut a greedy ambition? I am a person, not your booty! Let me go now, you misbegotten trollspawn!'

Starkad slapped her rump affectionately. 'Accept it. Your father the king and all his men are unable to rescue you. I shall take you back to my home in the world of men and there you shall submit to me.'

Reaching the head of the valley, he glanced back to see the city of the elves thronged with darting figures, like a forest anthill crushed by a booted foot. The elves seemed to be lacking in all direction. Some were following, but at a distance. He didn't think they posed much threat. He turned and ran through the trees, with Princess Alfhild's struggling form still slung over his shoulder.

As he did so, a drumming noise came from the clearing ahead and he saw a host of riders heading through the trees towards him. The man who led them wore a circlet upon his brow.

5: Princess Alfhild

S TARKAD RAN FOR the undergrowth, and flung himself down into a ditch, still holding the struggling princess, whose finery was smeared with Alfheim mud. He looked back over his shoulder. The riders galloped past oblivious.

'That is my father,' said Princess Alfhild in a muffled tone.

Starkad turned to see she had wriggled her face free from his enveloping palm. She might give the alarm. He slammed his hand back over her mouth, then tore a strip off her dress to gag her with. She got a hand free and scratched at his face. He tripped her with his leg and she fell with a splash into the ditch water. He rolled her over, and bound her slim arms behind her, then rolled her over again—she was covered top to toe in mud by now —and gagged her. Even so, she managed to sink a slender knee into his groin. He grunted.

By now the riders must be back at the city. If King Alf led them, and that certainly would explain the circlet the leader wore, then the elves would soon be better organised. He had to get back to the boat as soon as possible.

With a grunt, he heaved the princess back over

his shoulder, squelched back out of the ditch, and ran down the forest path, now churned up by fresh hoof prints.

He had got halfway to the coast, and the seas of darkness were visible through the trees, when his ears caught more drumming of hoofs from the distance, in the direction of the elfin city. He looked back but could see no sign of pursuit through the avenues of trees. Nonetheless, the sound of riders, shouted commands, the clatter of arms and armour pursued him. Were they too far off? Or—a horrible thought struck him—were they invisible? They were elves, after all.

He turned and ran on. At last he came down into the cove, Princess Alfhild still struggling on his shoulder. He deposited her in the bow, cut the painter, and steered a course for the sea of darkness. His paddles splashed in the water. Soon they were so far across the sea that Alfheim was no longer visible.

Princess Alfhild tried to kick him. He removed her gag. 'I'll untie you,' he said, ignoring the un-princess-like torrent of invective, 'if you promise to sit quietly and be a good girl.'

'This is an outrage!' she snarled. 'Turn about at once and return me to my father.'

Starkad left her lying in the scuppers, hands still bound, and went to inspect his caulking.

On they sailed across the dark sea, with little more than a breeze in the sails, enough to keep them sailing. Starkad tried to ask the princess if her people were sailors, but she proved unhelpful. There was no sign of pursuit, which surprised Starkad. He had only grabbed the golden goblets so he could fling them aside to slow down pursuers. He inspected one thoughtfully. It was an exquisite piece of work. He looked up. Despite her bedraggled appearance, the same could be said of Princess Alfhild. Her eyes met his and she gave him a look of pure hatred.

'It seems that your father doesn't love you as much as you thought,' he taunted her. 'Otherwise he would be after you by now.'

She looked away, as best as she could, lying in the scuppers with her hands tied behind her back. Starkad sat down beside her. 'Accept it,' he told her. 'You're my wife now.' He reached out to stroke her grimy cheek and she shrank away. 'I've won you by right of conquest.'

'I am not plunder,' she hissed. 'You cannot steal me. I am a princess of the elves, not a treasure hoard.'

'You're more precious and more beautiful than that,' the giant told her with heavy gallantry. She stared at him, eyes narrowed to slits, but this time she did not look away.

The seas of darkness gave way to more earthly oceans. Starkad survived the voyage by fishing. The fish had to be eaten raw since he had not been able to stock up on firewood at their previous landfall. The princess hated this, but Starkad told her that he was accustomed to such privations.

'You boast of your poverty?' she said, as he fed her by hand. As she gulped down a piece of raw, fresh fish, she made a moue of disgust.

'Hardiness,' Starkad corrected her. 'In the world of the giants, and even in that of men, I have lived a harsh, rugged life. It has made me manly, not an idle fop of the sort you know from Alfheim.'

'Why do you feel you have to impress me?' she fleered. 'You have me at your mercy. You don't need to boast about how tough you are, you've overpowered me. Who are you trying to convince? Me? Or yourself?'

Without replying, Starkad went and stood in the prow, gazing at the rise and fall of the waves as they sailed on towards the shores of Midgard.

She didn't seem to appreciate that he came from a tougher, manlier world than her own. The decadent delights of dancing and singing and feasting that had been her life so far were gone now. Now she was adrift in a savage world, where strength was needed to survive. Starkad had survived, because he was strong. He was ruthless. He took what he wanted. He had taken her! She should accept defeat, accept his superiority. And yet, even helpless and at his mercy, she had a tongue that was more wounding than the sharpest spear. He was at a loss as to how he should tame her.

One morning, he saw seagulls flocking off the starboard bow, and turned the vessel in that direction. Soon a line of clouds was visible on the horizon, and he knew that must mean landfall wasn't far off. The stars of the Midgard night had guided him for the last few days, and he was sure they were nearing the Telemark coast. Taking a sighting on the sun, he sailed north east.

A day later, they were ashore. Snjalli and his kin came to greet them.

'When you vanished in the night, Aludreng, we were afraid,' Snjalli confessed. 'We thought you had abandoned us. Where did you go?' He eyed Starkad's otherworldly prisoner doubtfully. Princess Alfhild looked a little better after Starkad had dangled her over the side to clean up the worst of the mud, but she was still disheveled and dispirited in appearance. 'Who is this strange female?' He noticed her bonds. 'A slave?'

'She is my wife, by right of conquest.' Starkad cut her bonds. 'This is Alfhild, princess of the elves.'

'You carried her off?' Snjalli said. 'Why, you have brought doom down upon us all! Her kindred will come seeking vengeance!'

'Her kindred are soft gutted pleasure seekers,' Starkad said, 'without the gumption to come after her. Isn't that right, wife? Your father has abandoned you.' He clapped the princess over her shoulder. 'Now you have no one in the world. Except me.'

When he struck her, she gave him an angry look. Now her hands were freed, she aimed a claw at him, but he grabbed her wrist and held her fast. Snjalli shook his head. 'There will be a reckoning for this, Aludreng, mark my words.'

Starkad paid him no heed. Taking Alfhild by the arm, he marched her up the valley to his cavern under the waterfall. Inside, Starkad found the wet nurse feeding Grim. She looked up placidly, and eyed the captive princess.

'You found your wife, then,' was all she said.

'Take care of her,' Starkad commanded, and pushed the princess in the thrall's direction. Leaving them to become acquainted, he stepped back through the curtain of water and surveyed his lands to see how they had fared during his absence.

Later he returned to find the princess transformed. The wet nurse had washed and stitched her tattered clothes and Alfhild herself had been bathed, had her hair brushed, and once again exuded that flowerlike scent. As Starkad entered the cavern, the elf maid was holding Grim, looking down into his entranced face and cooing.

'You like children?' said Starkad.

She looked up, her face serene. 'Yes,' she murmured. 'Is he yours?'

Starkad shook his head. 'His mother and father are dead. I am his foster father.'

She studied him enquiringly, still rocking the child. Starkad sent the wet nurse to the kitchen cave to prepare a homecoming meal.

'Who are you, who kills elf warriors without a qualm, who has abducted me and treated me shamefully, dragging me from world to world—and yet who fosters orphans?'

Starkad laughed. 'You'll learn there is more to me than meets the eye,' he said, 'now you are my wife. I may look like a monster, but I am a man.'

6: King Of The Elves

WHEN Alf, king of Alfheim, returned to his tree city of Gimle from making his offerings at the autumn sacrifice, he found all in disarray. There were signs of a massacre in the river meadows where his daughter liked to picnic with her maidens. Armed elves ran hither and thither, all seemingly on some urgent errand, but with no sign that anyone was in command. Other elves were running into houses, running out of houses, panicking, hiding. King Alf leapt down from his steed, flung the reins to a nearby guard, who dropped his spear and shield and stared at them in bewilderment.

The king leapt atop a tree stump and shouted, 'Silence!'

Gradually, the confusion died away. The running elves stopped running. The guards, apart from the one holding the horse's reins, formed up in orderly lines. Alf's riders reined their horses behind him. The citizens of Gimle gathered, talking amongst themselves until another shout from their king quietened them.

'What is happening here?' the king cried. 'My riders and I return from the autumn sacrifice to find all in chaos. Has an army attacked while we were offering to the gods?'

An elfin chamberlain hurried forward, his eyes wide. 'No army, sire!' he said. 'It was but one man that attacked! And...'

The king interrupted before the chamberlain could finish. 'One man? One man was capable of sacking my city in my absence?'

'A giant he was!' the chamberlain protested. 'An eight armed giant! Your guards tried to fight him but...'

'I have seen the bodies and the blood.' The king interrupted again. 'But where is this attacker's body? Surely you won't tell me he escaped after inflicting such losses on my city?'

The chamberlain looked ready to weep. 'Sire! He returned from whence he came, only moments ago. He went in that direction!' A trembling finger indicated the path down which the king and his riders had entered the valley. 'Surely you must have seen him! And sire...'

The king frowned. 'I saw no one.' He looked to his men for confirmation and they all shook their heads. 'He didn't go that way. What are these lies?'

'But sire...!' the chamberlain said. 'There is more!'

'What else? Tell me!' the king commanded.

'The giant who attacked the city...'

'Yes, go on!'

'He carried off the princess!'

The king stared at him in abject confusion.

'He abducted Alfhild, princess of Alfheim.'

In horror, the king looked back in the direction he had come from. They were close to the coast here, but they had never had to patrol the shore; few were rash enough to raid Alfheim. All knew that they had the favour of the gods. And yet this giant had invaded and carried off his daughter.

'He'll be too far away now,' said the king thoughtfully. 'Away across the seas of darkness.'

He turned back to the chamberlain. 'This city must be put into order at once!' he said. 'And call a council of the general assembly. This invasion must be discussed, as must be our response!'

He strode away to his hall.

The general assembly gathered on the plain outside the city. Present were representatives of all the trade guilds and the landholders and the warriors of Gimle and the surrounding countryside. The king faced them, and spoke sombrely.

'We have been attacked,' he said, 'by a foe from another world. It seems that one of the giants of Jotunheim or Trollheim has visited us. As I am sure you all know, this attack has hit me badly. He has carried off my daughter, who was accounted the most beautiful maiden in all the worlds. He also slew several of my guards and some minstrels.'

'We must ensure that in future my fellow musicians are protected from such attacks,' said the hirsute grandmaster of the minstrels' guild. Several of his fellow masters nodded in whiskery agreement.

'The guards also require assurances that they will be given full warning of such attacks ahead of time,' said the guard captain, a burly, scarred elf. 'We in Gimle have not been attacked for generations.' And elven generations were centuries of human time.

'You must be prepared for attack at any time!' the king said. He shook his head. 'It's my fault. In the long years of peace and prosperity that Frey has bestowed upon us, I have allowed you to go soft.' The guard captain looked angry.

A silk clad merchant piped up.

'What I want to know,' he said, 'is what steps will be taken to ensure that this never happens again? We should muster a war band at once and invade Jotunheim.'

'To avenge ourselves on a single rogue giant?' the guard captain said. 'Then we would have war with the giants. It would be a long, protracted conflict, in uncertain country. Besides, some of the giants are on the side of our allies the Aesir. We do not wish to alienate the Aesir, or the Vanir!'

'We should send a force in pursuit of this giant,' said a landowner. 'Hunt him down and kill him for what he has done. I would have thought you would be most keen to do this, sire,' he added, turning to the king, 'since the giant has carried off your beloved daughter.'

The king sighed. 'Trackers have found signs of where he went, and he must have passed by me by mere yards. They traced his flight through the forest to an inlet in the sea of darkness. A boat had been moored there, but it was long gone. So was the giant. So was my daughter. Where they went, who knows? Who can track a boat across the waters of the ocean?'

The guard captain shook his head. 'We elves have no skill as sailors,' he said. 'In the forest our trackers are the finest, but at sea...'

'No one but the most skilled of seers could track a fugitive across the seas of darkness,' said the merchant firmly. 'We need to make a show of strength. Enter the world of the giants with a war host and loot and burn. I will happily provide for the commissary needs of the army, at a discount, sire, and in return for a fifth share of any plunder...'

'We do not wish to make war with the giants,' the king stated. 'It is a war we could not win, and besides, we do not even know if the giant in question came from Jotunheim. Giants dwell in other worlds, including Midgard.'

'In Midgard?' said the captain, shocked. 'Surely Thor would not permit such a thing!' Thor was guardian of Midgard, just as Frey ruled over Alfheim.

'Thor...' said the king. 'Thor was much enamoured with my daughter, and wanted her as another wife...'

'Thor could track down this giant,' said the minstrel, 'and would avenge our indignity willingly. He slays giants for sport, and if we were to tell him that this one had ravished a girl he was fond of...'

'The thunder god would move heaven and earth to find the giant and rescue my daughter,' said the king. He looked pensive. 'This means I will have to accept him as my son in law. I would do so gladly, although my daughter is not so eager to join his harem...'

'Once she has been rescued from her abductor by Thor, she will see reason,' the landowner assured him.

'Then we must speak with him,' said the king. 'We will offer up a sacrifice to him. I shall pray to Thor at the height of the ritual, and bid him go out into the worlds to hunt down this malformed giant.'

'Do you think that even Thor could defeat him?' the captain asked. 'He is mighty, and has eight arms, so he wields four swords at once. That was why my men fell before him. Fighting him is like fighting four normal giants.'

The king brooded. 'If anyone can defeat him, it would be Thor.'

'Sire,' said the merchant, 'what if the giant...' He halted.

'What is it?' the king said impatiently. 'Go on!'

The merchant looked at the others. 'I was going to say, what if he has taken your daughter's maidenhood? Will Thor be so eager to rescue his intended if he knows she is no longer a virgin?'

The king tugged at his moustache. 'We shall not mention it to him,' he said at last. 'Not until it is necessary.'

He was filled with horror and disgust at the notion of his daughter naked in the arms of an eight armed murderous monster. And what would the children be like? Thank the gods his wife had died before this outraged occurred.

The full moon rose over the grove in the woods where stood the rune carved stone circle where from time immemorial the elves of Alfheim had sacrificed to their gods, the Aesir and Vanir. Hundreds of elves stood on the edges of the grove, holding torches as the oxen were led down the ceremonial way to the killing ground before the altar. The king stood beside the stone, holding the sacrificial poleaxe in his hand. Great cauldrons had been hung over blazing fires in which the meat of the oxen would be seethed before the elves feasted upon it in the name of their defender, Thor.

'Hail to the gods!' the king called up to the starry heavens. 'Hail to the goddesses! Hail to the holy powers!'

Two elves led the first ox to the king's side and he struck it with the poleaxe. It sank to its knees and the king slit its throat. The blood spurted out, spraying the altar, drenching it, and a coppery tang hung in the air. As soon as the ox had stopped moving, other elves hauled it over to the first of the cauldrons where they butchered it and thrust the meat into the bubbling liquid.

Ox after ox was led forward, each garlanded

with flowers. The king grew tired swinging his poleaxe, but even as his sinews ached, he thought of his daughter, a prisoner of that wicked giant, living in a cold, draughty cave in the world of men, and it fired his resolve. Blood pooled around his feet and still he slew oxen and still the elfin butchers filled the seething cauldrons with meat.

Now the king took a horn of mead and lifted it high, pointing it to the four quarters. 'I offer this mead in the name of Thor, defender of worlds, son of Odin, wielder of the hammer, crusher of the giants.' He poured the mead onto the ground. 'Come to us, I bid thee, and bring us your aid!' Thunder rumbled from a cloudless night sky and lightning split the darkness.

A chariot rumbled into the grove, driven by two huge goats. A gasp came from the assembled elves. The king quailed at the burly, bearded man who stood in the back of the vehicle. Over his shoulder he carried a large, short handled hammer. His eyes blazed fiercely, and his beard and long, plaited hair was red. His face was also ruddy. His body was massive, muscular, mighty.

He glared about him. 'I am Thor,' he bellowed. 'You called my name? Who are you?'

The king stepped forward. 'I, I am king of the elves,' he said. 'My daughter is Princess Alfhild.'

Thor stared at him, then laughed a booming laugh. He leapt down off his chariot and clapped the king over the shoulders. 'Hah ha!' he shouted. 'I know the girl! Leastways, I've seen her around. Bit of a looker, hey? I wouldn't mind her for my wife. Sif's annoyed. So's Jarnsaxa. But you can't be son of Odin without putting a few noses out of joint. Haughty little misses, them.'

He drew the king closer. 'She's not a nagger, is she?' he asked in a quieter voice. 'Don't like naggers. Got two already! Sometimes I think I'd rather wed my goats. Hah ha! Get it? Eh? Eh? Get it?' He slapped the king on the back.

When he had got his breath back, the king said, 'Certainly. I understand you. My, my wife was the same. No longer with us, of course.'

'Lucky you!' Thor boomed, and nudged him in the ribs. He halted, and peered round at the silent ranks of elves. 'What the Hel do they want?' he asked. While waiting for the king to reply, he thrust a ham-like fist into a bubbling cauldron and hauled out a hunk of ox meat. 'Well?' he added indistinctly, munching eagerly.

'They are my people, O Thor,' said the king. 'We gathered here to call upon you. To beseech for your aid.'

'Well!' said Thor. 'All you need do is ask. Though I thought Frey was your god.'

'Frey is indeed our god,' said the king, 'but as you know he is a god of peace. We need a god who knows how to fight.'

Thor stuck his thumbs into his belt and puffed out his chest. He tapped himself on the breastbone and grinned. 'You chose well, elf king,' he boomed. 'But what can I do for you?' His eyes narrowed. 'This isn't one of Loki's tricks, is it? I'm not going to be made to look a fool, am I?' He peered about him, genuinely concerned, then said, 'Nay, of course, my father fettered that little pest in a hell pit. So it's not Loki. What is it? Trolls that need hunting, first giants' skulls to crush? Hey, where is your little girl?'

'It is to do with a giant, yes,' said the king. 'An eight armed giant. And with my little girl. She's been abducted.'

'No!' said Thor in wonder. 'Who is it who's had the gall to run off with Thor's intended? I'll break his bastard bones for him! I'll rip off those arms of his!' He pounded one mighty fist into another. 'I'll go straight to the world of giants and find him and then I'll kill him!'

The king smiled slyly. 'I was rather hoping you'd say that.'

7: God Of Thunder

STARKAD SAT PEACEFULLY in the sun beside the waterfall, watching Alfhild in the meadow, playing with young Grim as best she could, waddling as she was from her pregnant belly. It was almost a year since he had carried her off from her own world. She had softened towards him, though he didn't think she loved him. She had accepted the situation. And there had been no repercussions, no attempts by her elfin kin to seek vengeance. Not that he had thought there would be.

At first Grim had occupied her time, and she had shared the wet nurse's duties in caring for him. Ogn's son was constantly getting himself into trouble. He was aggressive for his age, something that Alfhild forgave, although she ascribed it to his trollish blood and his early upbringing.

Rising to his feet, Starkad lumbered over to join them.

The moment his dark, malformed shadow fell over them, Grim toddled to his feet and waved a fist at his foster father. Alfhild gave him a disapproving frown. 'You scare him,' she said accusingly.

Starkad was troubled. 'I did naught,' he protested. 'I only came over to join you.'

Alfhild shook her head. 'A troll like you knows naught of fatherhood,' she muttered, and looked away.

Her eyes brightened. 'Look! Here comes the wet nurse.'

Starkad saw the Lapp girl trudging up the hill path. She had been sent to the village earlier to get eggs and meal, and she carried a basket under one arm. Seeing her master and mistress watching her, she hurried up. Soon she was with them. Alfhild took the supplies from the wet nurse, who welcomed the embrace of Grim. Starkad watched the happy domestic scene darkly. It seemed he could never connect with his family and dependents.

'I talk to Snjalli's wife,' the wet nurse said. 'She say wandering witch come to village. Conjured spirits, told people's fortunes. Said Snjalli's son would be happy and prosperous and die an old man in his bed.'

Alfhild beamed broadly. Her people were fascinated by magic and witchcraft.

She turned to her husband. 'We should ask her to stay the night with us,' she said. 'She is still in the neighbourhood?' she asked the wet nurse, who nodded. 'There, husband! We should invite her here before she goes on her way!'

Starkad scowled. He didn't approve of troubling spirits or raising ghosts.

'No man can know his fate,' he muttered. 'And to die a straw death in old age will mean an afterlife in Hel's cold kingdom.'

'But wouldn't you want to know?' Alfhild asked. 'Don't you want to know what will be Grim's fate?' She rested her hand on her pregnant belly. 'Or Storvirk—or Baugheid?' She had settled on both a name for a girl and a name for a boy.

Starkad could not believe he would father anyone other than a boy. 'What if his fate was a terrible one?' he asked. 'What if he learnt that he was fated to die of sickness or disease?'

Alfhild pouted, and frowned. 'Naught like that will happen to my baby,' she said. 'Please, husband.' She reached out and stroked one of his arms. 'Please!'

Starkad shook his head obstinately.

But that night, much to Starkad's displeasure, Alfhild invited the witch to his subterranean hall behind the waterfall. He sat in his elaborately carved chair, a dark expression on his face, his many hands gripping its arms as the firelight red lit an eerie scene.

The witch, whose name was Huld, was a plump, middle aged woman who spoke in a scatter-brained fashion, her lips forever in a fatuous smile. Starkad's own lips were thin as he looked on the proceedings in distaste.

Alfhild sat on a rug, Grim in her lap, resting his little head on her belly. The wet nurse watched keenly. The witch chanted strange, uncanny words. Starkad thought that such sights were not suitable for children.

Now the witch sat back, her head against the back of the platform she had erected. She ceased her chant gradually, her words drifting away from her lips. Now her eyes rolled upwards in their sockets, as if she was trying to see the inside of her own skull. For a moment she sat there in silence.

'Too much mead,' Starkad scoffed. 'She's fallen asleep.' Assuming she hadn't died, he told himself. But that was too much to hope for.

His wife gave him a disapproving look. She put her fingers to her lips.

'Don't distract her!' she hissed. 'You'll break her trance.'

'Trance!' Starkad said. 'She's dead drunk, that's all. You were too generous with that mead.'

Before Huld had begun her chanting, or taken over Starkad's dais, she had demanded a meal, including a porridge made of the hearts of all animals available. Alfhild had managed to find a pig's heart and a lamb's heart, although the witch had seemed to think this inadequate. However, she had tucked in with a will, and washed it down with half a jug full of mead.

It looked like an easy enough life to Starkad. To wander the land swindling housewives with tales of fortune telling and conjuring, getting a free meal in every household. His fingers itched to give the fraud of a witch a good thrashing, the whipping such impudent beggars deserved, and put her out of the cave with speed. He gave his wife a glare, but she wasn't looking at him anymore.

Huld's mouth gaped open and she yawned cavernously. Starkad snorted. 'What did I say? She's gone to sleep!'

Alfhild's brow furrowed. 'Be silent!' she said. 'She's not asleep. She has sent her soul out into the otherworld. Do you know naught of witchcraft?'

Starkad was certain the woman had simply gone to sleep. He resented her wife's superior airs. This nonsense was just that. The witch had got herself drunk at his own expense and now she had fallen asleep!

Then her eyes rolled back down and she stared forwards, apparently unseeingly. Her voice opened again.

'She sees a boy, a boy who is an orphan, mother and father dead by violence.'

Alfhild clutched at Grim's shoulders and the little boy gurgled happily. 'She means you,' she hissed.

'Anyone could have told her Grim's an orphan,' Starkad said. 'Besides, what does she mean, "She sees"?'

Alfhild gave him another glare. 'Everyone knows that spaewives speak of themselves like that. Sssh! She has more to say.'

'She sees a boy,' the witch repeated, 'a boy grown to manhood, though still young. He sails into the storm. Riches and renown are his; he weds his foster sister.

'She sees, further down the stream of time, a dwarf forged, cursed sword...' The witch broke off and stared unseeingly into the distance.

Alfhild looked unbelievingly at Grim. 'Does she mean that our foster son will marry our daughter?' she asked.

'Daughter!' Starkad sneered. 'She's making it up! We'll have a son.'

And now the witch had gone silent again. Dreaming up more lies, no doubt, Starkad thought.

Alfhild shook her head. 'It is possible,' she said. 'Maybe I bear a daughter. They may well become close.' She looked excited. 'But did you hear? Riches and renown!' Then she looked troubled. 'Although I don't like the idea of him sailing the sea. That sounds dangerous.'

Starkad barked with laughter. 'How else is the lad to get riches and renown if he doesn't seize it with all his hands? That's how I got mine.'

Alfhild sniffed and looked round the cave. 'I'd like to think he could become wealthy as a landowner or merchant,' she sad. 'What's wrong with that?' she added as Starkad snorted. 'Plenty of men have become wealthy through trade.'

'And what name have they won for themselves?' Starkad asked. 'The name of coward. Is that what you want for Grim?'

Alfhild looked pensive. 'I don't want him taking after his father, or his foster father either,' she said.

Starkad grunted. 'Has this hag any more to add?' he demanded. 'Or has she gone to sleep again?'

'I thought you weren't interested in what she had to say,' Alfhild said snidely.

Starkad sat back. 'I'm not,' he said. But he had become interested despite himself. He wanted to hear more.

Huld's mouth gaped again. Again she yawned. The cave was so quiet that the hiss of her escaping breath was audible despite the crackle of the fire and the distant roar of the waterfall.

'She sees...' came the susurrus of breath, 'she sees a boy...'

'Not again,' said Starkad.

'Sssh!' said Alfhild.

'She sees a boy... whose mother hates her father,' Huld said at last.

Starkad stared at Alfhild. The elf refused to look at him, but clasped her hands as if protectively over her big belly.

'She sees his blood runs pure,' Huld went on; 'she sees him conceived in anger. She sees him follow in his father's footsteps...'

Starkad sat up. Was this his son? 'She sees a hall in flames, screaming women...' Alfhild nodded bitterly. '...a woman slain by vengeful brothers...' Starkad shook his head. This made no sense. 'She sees the seed of evil sown, not burnt by fire. It grows. It blossoms.' She paused, then added, 'It is here.'

'What?' Starkad said, looking around in puzzlement. 'It's here? Where?'

'...it will be reborn...' Huld's eyes rolled back in their sockets.

Starkad stared at Alfhild. 'What does she mean?'

'Evil is here,' said Alfhild.

'Where?' Starkad said. 'Where is this evil? I see naught.'

'I thought you didn't believe,' Alfhild replied sulkily.

Starkad laughed. 'Of course I don't,' he said. 'I just want to know what she means when she says that evil is here.'

'Isn't it obvious?' Alfhild cried. 'You're evil. Anyone can see that.'

Starkad stared at her, wounded. After a long silence, during which the fire crackled and the falls thundered in the distance, and the witch's breathing wheezed on, and Grim nodded in Alfhild's arms, he said, 'Does my unborn son's mother really hate his father?'

Alfhild looked away. 'I don't know,' she said. 'I... sometimes I do. Why shouldn't I? I, I thought you didn't believe in this.'

'Maybe not,' he said, 'but I want to hear more from her. We've heard about the children, although it made little sense. But what of us? What of you? What... what of me?'

'Why don't you ask her?' said Alfhild viciously. 'Oh, but you don't believe in witchcraft, do you? Shall I ask for you? Are you too afraid? Are you frightened of what you will learn of your own future? Would you prefer it that you never knew?'

'I don't want to know my fate,' Starkad said contemptuously. But he did. He wanted to know what would happen to him. 'What of your own fate? What will happen to my wife?' he asked the witch.

'She sees an elfin girl, freed from drudgery,' Huld wheezed. 'She sees happiness when there was sorrow. She sees love where once was hate...'

Leaping from his seat Starkad struck the witch across the face. Alfhild cried out in protest. Huld's eyes snapped back in her head and she looked venomously at him. Grim woke, crying.

Huld dabbed at her bruised cheek. She looked up. 'Nay, dear,' she said. 'Don't castigate your man. He will pay for his crimes. She sees...!'

Above the distant crash of the falls, came a boom of thunder.

Thor rode his chariot across the moonlit sky. Down below, he saw where the craggy land met the crashing waves of the sea. Great fjords had nibbled the shores in many places. Here the Bones of Ymir lay close to the surface, the great stone skeleton of the cosmic giant who Thor's father Odin had slain in the morning of the world. Thor himself had not been born in those days. And yet it was Jord, the goddess of the earth, who had been his mother.

He had been searching Midgard for some while

now, having abandoned his quest in the world of the giants as fruitless. No word of Starkad or his people had he got from friendly giants, except that he had defeated Gudmund's people and demanded his daughter as his wife as part of the peace settlement. Gudmund disowned the girl, and he had heard no more of her. A shame.

From what Thor had heard of Ogn, she would make an impressive addition to his collection of wives. Still, Princess Alfhild, Starkad's latest prey, was of more importance—and greater beauty, from what Thor had heard of Ogn's beauty. Alfhild's was undeniable. That was why he had chosen her for his new wife. He wondered what he would do if the girl had fallen for Starkad. But that was impossible, not when she knew Thor loved her.

'There!' he bellowed to the goats that drew his chariot, seeing a valley far below. 'That is where they said he has his cave! Go down!'

The chariot began to descend. Thor shook his hammer and thunder boomed from the livid clouds, while blue white lightning crackled down at the ground far below.

Filthy cave dwelling troll. To infest a mountain on Midgard, the world Thor had sworn to protect, and to pose as some kind of god to the people who dwelt nearby! The world was a big place, and even gods could not keep their eyes on all that happened—except Odin. Despite his missing eye, Odin could see everywhere, or at least his ravens could. But he kept his own counsel. He had never warned his son that this deformed giant had taken up residence in a Midgard cave.

The mountain peaks drew ever nearer, very sharp, like needles below. The valley opened up between them. It was night. Thor could see very little. But there was a river, its foaming stream visible in the moonlight. Along its side as it wound towards the sea was a small village. And further up the mountainside was a waterfall.

At last they touched down in the meadow beside the roaring falls. Thor jumped down from his chariot, gripping his hammer in his gauntleted hands. He took a pace closer to the waterfall, standing on the edge of the sloping meadow.

'Come out!' he boomed. 'Come out now, trollspawn! Ravisher of women! Come out and meet your match!'

For a moment there was silence, broken only by the roar of the falls.

'Come out!' Thor shouted. 'Or shall I come in and get you?'

Then he saw a grey figure looming amid the water. At last it came out, wading through the stream and onto dry land. Thor's lip curled at the huge, malformed shape.

'Who challenges Starkad?' the giant demanded. In four of his eight hands he held unsheathed swords. Thor laughed.

'Who challenges you? Weep on your knees, trollspawn!' he boomed. 'For I am Thor! I am the vanquisher of many of your kin!'

'Your father slew Ymir,' Starkad noted, stomping towards him, swords glinting in the moonlight. 'You are known for hunting giants for sport. It will be a pleasure to slay you, Thor.'

Thor laughed again, and whirled his hammer. Starkad raced across the intervening turf, swords swinging from every direction. Thor reached out with his left gauntleted fist, seized one blade and shattered it with a squeeze. At the same time, he brought his hammer in low, smashing Starkad's thighbone.

Starkad gasped with pain, and went down on one knee. He dropped the sword that Thor had broken, upturned another to lean on it, then stabbed up at the looming thunder god with a third, trying to get his belly. In an electric crackle, Thor swung his hammer round and parried the blow. As hammer met sword, sparks cascaded across the turf, a fiery likeness of the waterfall behind them. But this was what Starkad had been expecting. He lunged with the last remaining sword, straight at Thor's heart.

With a roar, Thor leapt back, but still Starkad's sword pierced his fur jacket, wounding him shallowly in the breastbone. Thor gripped his belt of might. His eyes flashed like the lightning, his beard bristled, and he advanced, swinging his hammer. Starkad tried to rise, but his broken leg gave under him, and Thor's hammer smashed his skull.

With a thud, his great carcase fell to the turf.

Hammer over his shoulder, one gauntleted hand in his belt, Thor studied the slaughtered giant with a grin of satisfaction. He stirred the corpse with his booted foot. When there was no response, he hung his hammer from his belt, seized one of Starkad's arms and tore it from its socket.

As he fulfilled his vow a small group appeared from the waterfall. One of them was a lithe elfin form he knew. Flinging the last of Starkad's arms down on the gory turf beside his chariot, he went to meet her.

His ruddy face fell as he saw the princess' companions. One was some kind of thrall woman, which was fine. But the thrall and the princess brought with them a toddler, who clung to the thrall's skirts. The lad was too old to be progeny of Alfhild and the late Starkad. But Thor also saw a prominent bulge in the princess' belly.

'Yes. I bear Starkad's child, Thor,' Princess Alfhild affirmed. 'And you are the killer of its father.'

Thor rested his hammer on his shoulder and raked Alfhild with his fiery glance. 'You're damaged goods, lass,' he told her levelly. 'I'm the eldest son of Odin. I wouldn't keep you as a mistress, let alone wed you.'

He turned, mounted his chariot, and with a rumble of thunder and a flash of lightning took off into the storm-wracked night sky.

Alfhild went back to her father and she took Grim with her. In Alfheim she gave birth to twins; a son called Storvirk and a daughter named Baugheid. When Grim was twelve, he became a Viking and gained many riches and much renown, after which he married Baugheid and they settled down on the island of Bolm, in Lake Bolm in Sweden, from which he became known as 'Eygrim', or Island-Grim. They had a son named Arngrim the Berserk and he was famous in later years, and bore the cursed sword Tyrfing.

Storvirk was dark haired and good-looking, taller and mightier than most men. He also became a great Viking and later joined the warband of Harald, king of Agder, rising in his service to become land-warden. Harald gave him Thruma Island where Storvirk had an estate.

Storvirk abducted Unn, daughter of Earl Freki of Halogaland, and they had a son who was named Starkad after his grandfather.

His story will also be told.

FROM THE SAGA OF STARKAD THE OLD

STARKAD THE REBEL

Prologue

A S THE SUN sank over the forests of the mainland, shadows pooled around the outbuildings and the quiet of dusk spread across the yard. The hall, its fantastically carven, brightly painted gables thrusting defiantly towards the descending darkness, resounded with the sound of rejoicing while red gold firelight spilled out onto the ground beyond the porch. The lord of the island was celebrating the name fastening of his little son, and all his family and hearthmen, and folk from throughout the kingdom, had come to the feast; ships rode at anchor in the firth below. He was a powerful man, land warden of the king, and folk for leagues around paid him due deference and tribute.

But outside, in the growing darkness, where even the thralls had shut up the cowsheds and pigsties and settled in for the night, stealthy, dark figures were moving. Anchored on the seaward side of the island was a longship bearing the raven standard of Halogaland, a kingdom of the distant north. But no one had seen them, no one had asked why they were anchoring so furtively on the coast of an island in the kingdom of Agder.

Now their crews had disembarked and were

making their way up through the pines that swathed the sides of the island. The vanguard had reached the edges of the fields, and now the fire-light and torchlight from the distant hall was the only illumination except the dim glimmer of the evening star. There was no moon. The men's spears and axes betrayed no glancing sheen. Their foot-steps were almost inaudible as they settled into position outside the hurdle fences, eyes fixed on the firelit hall. Tonight, a different fire would light the hall of Storvirk, land warden of Agder.

At last, all the warriors were in place. It was now black as Hel. Still no moon had risen, and only starlight bathed the sward in a dim, eerie silver. This night had been well chosen. The two noble brothers who led this expedition conferred in a murmur from their place at the centre of the line of warriors. Still the roar of festivities troubled the night air, but at the edge of the wind twisted trees all was silent except the sigh of the breeze among the pines and the whispers of the two brothers. Their men were well disciplined, well-schooled warriors who knew how to keep silent and still while carrying out a night attack.

The two brothers lay among the pine needles, planning their strategy. It was so dark beneath the trees that only their eyes could be seen, and their teeth when they bared them in savage, wolfish grins. The man who held this island in fealty to Harald, king of Agder, had done their kindred wrong, and they were resolved to settle with steel the score that their enemy had left unpaid when he visited their sister's bower in icy Halogaland.

'They think themselves invulnerable to attack,' said Fjori with a grin. 'For a man whose king made him land warden, our enemy makes a poor show of guarding his own boundaries.'

Apart from a couple of fights with enemy ships, which had ended with their foes sent to the bottom, the warband had reached the island unmolested. Their advance scouts had met a patrol in the forest while spying out the way, but after a brief skirmish they had killed most, and taken the remaining two captive. Some whittle work with hot iron had wrung a few answers from the prisoners' lips, and now their bodies floated facedown in the firth.

'He thinks he can raid our own lands with impunity,' said his brother Fyri, bitterly. 'He thinks he can carry off our sister to be his wife and pay no bride price. Folk say he comes of the blood of trolls. Tonight, we teach this trollspawn a stern lesson.'

'And by Thorgerd Holgabrud, our whore of a sister must also die,' Fjori replied. 'She has brought dishonour upon our kin. Show no mercy. We shall bolt the doors from the outside so Storvirk does not get a chance to kill us, then burn down the hall around their heads. No quarter even for women and bairns.' Lightly, to avoid too much noise, he smacked his gauntleted fist into his palm. 'We restore Halogaland's honour tonight.'

Within the hall, all was festive and cheerful. Merry laughter and chatter reached to the high cruck beams and the shield- and banner-hung pillars half lit by the flickering light of the fire trenches that bisected the floor, offering welcome heat in the draughty space and a means to roast the vast carcases of oxen and swine that gave the chattering multitude meat. Torches blazed lower down on the ornately carved pillars, throwing ruddy light on the magnificent wall hangings that twitched in the warm air and smoke.

Between the fire trenches and beneath the cruck beams of the hall, three long trestle tables sat many men and women, the pristine white tablecloths gradually besmirched with spilt ale, mead and wine, meat and broth. Up on the dais was the high table at which sat the lord and lady of the house, the latter bearing in her arms the swaddled figure of a baby which she had taken from a nurse who stood beside her.

She cradled her little son in her arms and looked up with a shy smile at her lord. 'Isn't he beautiful? What are we going to call him?'

He took the bairn from her and wrapped it in the folds of his red cloak. Grimly, he parted the swaddling clothes. 'We must see that he is whole, wife,' he said. 'Before the folk, we shall show that he has no malformities. Of course, if he does...'

She gripped his arm. 'No! He is our son!'

He prised her hand away. 'Aye! If he is truly deformed, he must be exposed, left to die in the open. It is the only way!' Her lord inspected the bairn remorselessly.

Unn, daughter of Earl Freki of Halogaland, bit her lip. She regretted her folly now, running away with a passing Viking, even if he was an important man in his own southern kingdom. So much had she sacrificed for his sake, throwing away her power and position in her own land for the sake of this dark haired, handsome man, about whom hung so many sinister rumours. At least he had given her a bairn—the boy, yet nameless, upon whom her happiness depended. And yet he was willing to cast that away for reason of ancient custom. Couldn't the custom be broken?

Silence had fallen over the feasters as all waited Storvirk Starkadsson's verdict.

'Look!' he murmured. 'See these? These marks?'

Anxious, Unn leaned forward. Storvirk held the bairn up in his unfeeling hands, naked and cold in the torchlight. She remembered the tales she had heard after coming to this country. That her husband's own father had been a malformed troll or giant, that he had carried off the princess of the elves as his wife, that she had been Storvirk's unwilling mother. He was of uncanny kin. He was barely human. No wonder he was so obsessed by the notion that his son would be deformed.

'Those?' she said, peering at the three circular puckers on the baby's side. She had already seen them, of course. They filled her with dread. 'They're just birthmarks, surely.'

She saw that another three were on the other flank, exactly adjacent. Her heart pounded. Deformed! And through no fault of her own. Her husband's trollish blood was clear in this. And now her bairn would be left out on the hillside to become the prey of wolves and carrion birds.

Storvirk shook his head. He held high the bairn, brandishing it at the gathered folk. 'It is a sign of his heritage!'

'His troll blood?' she said angrily, defensively, dread in her heart. 'And where does this taint originate? I? Or you?'

He gave her an uncomprehending look. 'He will grow up to be a true man of my blood,' he said, and with a shock of joy Unn realised he was pleased. 'He bears on his flanks the marks where my father's many arms grew. These are no malformities but a sign that he shall grow up to be a great warrior. This confirms it. There is naught for it but to name his for his grandsire.'

Taking up a cup from the table, he splashed water on the baby's face, who bore this assault with dignity. 'I name thee, lad, Starkad.'

'What's that smell?' Unn said suddenly. She broke off in a fit of coughing.

Outside the hall, thralls fled their huts as the Halogalander warriors surrounded the great hall of Storvirk. Contemptuously the men ignored the running figures except to cut them down if they came too close. Most escaped into the woods. Behind them they left a hall that was catching flame. The brothers' men held blazing torches to the dry hall timbers and thatch and now smoke was twining its way up into the night sky where a gibbous moon had now risen. Even as Fjori Frekisson watched, he saw to his satisfaction that it was beginning to burn heartily now.

He and his brother stood with their huskarls before the main doors of the hall, from which the muted sounds of festivity filtered. But even as he listened, the table laughter turned to lamentation as the hall burned.

'Get ready,' he said to his men. Sure enough, moments later, the first figure came stumbling out through the doors, coughing and spluttering in the smoke that billowed after it. It was a stripling, the worse for drink, eyes wide in fear for his life. But the real threat stood at his side, with a drawn longsword. It came slashing down, and the fleeing youth fell at the feet of one of Fjori's huskarls.

Others came after the youth, coughing and choking, but the Halogalanders rushed forward to cut them down, then bolted the doors from without. For now, the flood of fugitives was stemmed. Silence fell broken only by the crackle of flames as the fire licked at the gables and a distant coughing from within. A blazing timber fell from the hall and landed a few feet from where Fjori stood.

A voice boomed from the hall. 'Who are the men without? What feud brings you to the hall of Storvirk Starkadsson?'

'Why,' Fjori cried in reply, 'it is your in-laws

come a visiting, trollspawn. We bring gifts of steel and flame. Come out here and we will load you down with our generosity.'

After a pause, another voice spoke shrilly from within the hall, a voice both brothers knew well.

'Would you kill your own brother in law? Your sister? Your nephew?'

Fyri looked at Fjori. 'It is Unn,' he said unnecessarily.

'No sister of mine,' Fjori shouted, 'is within this hall. Only a whore who ran off with a troll spawned Viking. They and any brat they might have spawned will die in flame or on my sword point. Thus shall the honour of Halogaland be restored.'

Within the hall was a scene of confusion. The less valiant of the guests had rushed to the doors, piling out through the porch until it became clear that death lay without as well as within. Smoke hung heavy in the air. The light of flames from the blazing walls and roof timbers washed the interior with a ghastly blood red. Unn coughed weakly as the smoke entered her lungs. She cradled her newly named son to her breast and looked around her at her panicking companions. Only her husband stood still and imperturbable on the dais.

He stepped down now and went to the doors, stalking through the smoke like a giant in the mists of Niflheim.

'Permit my guests and hearth-men to depart,' Storvirk bellowed. 'They have no part in our feud.'

From outside came the familiar voice of Fjori. 'You shall all die in there. We won't let anyone escape. We shall extinguish your monstrous line.'

Eyes streaming with tears—from the smoke, not from fear—Unn turned to the nurse. 'Listen, girl,' she said. 'Is there another way out of this hall?'

'You mean to flee?' the girl asked.

Unn shook her head. 'And abandon my lord? No, I'll face whatever he confronts. No. I wish that my son survives us—to gain vengeance, if naught else. If you know any way to escape this place, take my son'—her heart panged her within her breast as she handed over the swaddled baby— 'and ensure he is raised as becomes his lineage.'

The nurse accepted the little bundle. 'There is a way,' she whispered, 'through the kitchens. I'll take it.'

Storvirk had been organising his hearth-men and guests, those who had not passed out due to the smoke, into a fighting force. By now the smoke was thick and timber beams fell blazing in sparks from the cruck beams. Bodies lay about the floor, some still living, gasping in the smoke, or struggling against fallen beams. One wall was a glowing mass of embers.

'Get your backs into it, men,' he urged them. 'We'll smash down this burning wall and then out into the yard and attack the Halogalanders.'

'But they outnumber us,' a man told him. 'There are so few of us left able to fight...' he broke off into a fit of coughing as another beam smashed down behind them, filling the air with ash and sparks.

'The fewer we are, the harder must we fight,' Storvirk intoned, but already the roof was falling, rendering his noble words futile.

Unn settled back at the high table, watching their struggles from the dais. A sense of finality, of inevitability, pressed down on her like a physical weight, as heavy as a fallen rafter. She looked round to see no sign of the nurse. She had done her duty. As the hall fell around them in fire and sparks, she sat patiently at the high table and awaited the end.

'It burns,' Fyri murmured. 'None try to flee. They are brave!'

'Or overcome by smoke,' Fjori replied. 'Only a coward accepts the inevitable rather than meeting death sword in hand.'

By morning, the hall, and the steading buildings surrounding it, were charred wrecks. Like swine, the Halogalanders rooted among the ruins, snatching what plunder had survived the inferno. The interior of the hall was littered with charred bodies. None were recognisable.

A warrior shouted out excitedly, pointing to a fallen timber, and Fjori joined him to see a girl's body some way from the hall, crushed by a charred rafter. For a moment, he thought it was his sister, that she still lived. But no. This girl, clad in the drab linen garments of a thrall, was a stranger. To one side, just out of reach of her outstretched white hand, lay a bundle of some kind. No doubt worthless trinkets of the sort a fleeing thrall would snatch. But they would not avail her. She was as dead as the rest.

As Fyri led the warrior away in search of richer pickings, the bundle twitched slightly.

Full to bursting with pride at their victory, ship packed with plunder, bellies sloshing with mead and ale, the Vikings sailed north towards their own kingdom.

'We avenged the shame Storvirk did us, eh, brother?' Fyri said, passing Fjori a skin of mead.

Fjori drank deep, and wiped his lips with the back of his hand. Exhilarated with the wind and the spray and the mead, he clung to a line and grinned. 'That we did,' he said. 'The coward died under our assault, and that whore of a sister is slain too. Her dishonour is wiped out by our valiant deeds!'

Fyri took the skin back from his brother and drank from it. They had a good wind and it was driving them north along the fjord bitten coast. The crew hung from the rigging or lazed on the salt sprayed deck. An air of celebration was almost tangible.

Despite his words Fjori was troubled by memories of his sister, and he grew maudlin, gazing over the side. She'd been a beautiful girl. Their mother would miss her, of course; that old woman had no real notion of honour. But there had been no other way. Unn had run away with a Sutherling Viking, casting shame on the family, on the realm. But they had avenged that slight. None had been left alive. None would dare cross the Halogalanders when news of this was heard among the deep fjords and the cold hillsides.

1: The Fosterling

SMOKE DRIFTED INTO the hazy blue skies of early afternoon and the air was rank with the stink of wet charcoal. It had been raining heavily when King Harald's slender longship set out from the shore on the king hearing news of the surprise attack upon Storvirk's steading—unprecedented, out of raiding season. The king had brought all his household with them, although they had remained in the vessel under guard until men returned from scouting to report that the raiders had gone. Now the rainstorm was over. The king and his retinue had reached the burnt remains of the steading and they were searching for signs of any survivors.

Queen Geirhild stood with her handmaidens and the young boy, Vikar. She was the king's second wife, and had for a time suffered a rival, Signy, daughter of the king of Voss. Often, she felt out of place among these nobles, coming as she did from a humbler background. Her fine looks and her skill in ale brewing had saved her from becoming the wife of some churl. Now her rival had been put away and she was the king's only wife, mother of his son.

She watched as her husband and his men inspected the ruins. At first, she had turned little Vikar's head away, thinking the scene unsuitable for such a tender bairn, but Harald had sternly forbidden her from mollycoddling the boy, and now Vikar stared at the half-burnt bodies with big eyes. Eager, he wanted to go and help his father inspect the ruins, but Queen Geirhild felt she could legitimately restrain him from this, however much he wriggled in her arms. He was a strong bairn, bound to grow up to be as strong a man like his father.

'You mustn't,' she told him. 'You'll get ash all over your best clothes!'

'Did they kill Father's friend?' Vikar asked, looking up at her with big eyes. 'Why did they do it, Mother? I don't understand.'

'We don't know what happened here, Vikar,' she said. 'Word only reached your father this morning. Sometimes men come up from the sea and attack folk's houses to rob them.' She failed to mention that in times of war his father did much the same.

'But why?' he demanded. 'When I'm king I won't let them.' This was a regular refrain these days, whenever Vikar met something he didn't understand or that he disliked. From what the queen could see, the boy would grow up to become either a paragon of virtue and justice or the worst tyrant since Ymir the frost giant.

Before she could answer, there was a commotion from the men. King Harald crouched down over a half-burnt corpse. Queen Geirhild put her slim hand to her mouth as the king seized it by its locks and rolled it over. She looked away, gagging, as he peered into the blackened face.

'What's wrong, Mother?' asked her unfeeling brute. 'You've gone awfully pale.'

'It's him,' announced King Harald, standing up dolefully. 'My land warden. He'll guard the land no longer.' He gestured to a huskarl with the order to take care of the charred corpse, and surveyed the dismal scene of wreck and ruin. 'As you know, I was unable to attend this banquet due to affairs of state.' The men all nodded seriously. Queen Geirhild knew that the real reason he had not attended was because he deemed it beneath his dignity to attend the festivities of his troll-spawned bondsmen, but she kept mum. 'But many of my chief men in the kingdom were here. We have lost many due to this unexpected attack.'

'What of the king's baby boy, milord?' Queen Geirhild called out. 'It was his name fastening that you couldn't attend.'

King Harald strode through the ruins, kicking idly at twisted, blackened metal, and fallen timbers. 'I doubt a babe survived where so many men died. And had we attended, perhaps little Vikar would be lying stark and dead somewhere on this field of slaughter.'

He bent down and beckoned to his boy, who disengaged himself from his mother's clutches and came running across the ground, dodging between warriors, towards his father. Queen Geirhild cried out when his foot struck a snag and he fell flat on the charred earth.

A muffled wail split the quiet. Queen Geirhild rushed forwards. King Harald scowled, shaking his head.

'Stop that grizzling!' he barked, as Vikar struggled to rise. 'You're the son of the king of Agder!'

Two warriors hurried forwards to help Vikar to his feet but the queen thrust herself between them and snatched up her boy. But Vikar's face showed not so much as a tearstain. He had tripped over a dirty bundle on the ground which lay close to the stiffened white hand of a dead serving girl. To her surprise, it was moving. A small pink object probed out of the bundle, tiny beige tentacles splaying at its end. She recognised it almost at once as a baby's arm.

Putting Vikar back on his feet, she crouched down again and picked up the swaddled bundle. Parting its folds, she saw an angry, squalling red face peering out. Love gushed up irresistibly into her heart.

She turned, smiling, to her husband as he forced his way through the gathered men. 'It's a babe!' she said. 'It must be Storvirk's baby boy!'

King Harald stroked his long dark beard and looked disapprovingly from beneath bushy brows. 'It'll die soon,' he predicted gloomily. 'No brat so small could survive being left on the ground overnight. Surprising wolves and foxes haven't torn him to pieces yet.'

Ignoring him, Queen Geirhild bounced the screaming bairn. She showed him to Vikar who looked at the shouting red thing critically. 'A brother for you!' she gushed.

'Why?' he said. 'What's it called, anyway?' Queen Geirhild looked at the king, who shook his head indifferently.

'My land warden said if the baby was a boy he was going to name it after his father. Starkad.'

'Starkad!' Queen Geirhild held the baby up to her face, as if to kiss him. Little Starkad lashed out with a tiny fist and caught her a blow on the end of her nose. King Harald and Vikar burst out laughing.

Geirhild sniffed, and rubbed her sore nose. Gathering the tatters of her dignity, she said, 'I see he'll grow up to be as much a brute as most men in this country. Well, at least some good has come out of all this destruction. I suggest you have these remains taken back to their kin for their funerals and return to your palace. Starkad will need a wet nurse, and some decent things.'

She swept away, followed by her husband and son. King Harald paused to give the orders to his hearth-men, his heart heavy with the knowledge that he had lost important men here, and then with a long face he went with his folk back to his vessel moored in the firth.

Although the identity of the attackers remained a mystery, over the next few years the story of the slaughter of King Harald's land warden and his guests spread far and wide, soon passing beyond the borders of the petty kingdom of Agder.

It came to the ears of the king of Hordaland, a realm many leagues up the coast, about half-way between Agder and Halogaland, home of the raiders. At this time, about a score of petty king-doms and independent earldoms flourished along the sea coast between the uninhabited mountains of the interior and the open ocean, the sea route known to sailors as the North Way, or Norway. At any given time, most of these kingdoms were at war with at least one of its rivals. Hordaland was no exception, and its king, Herthjof, grandson of the far famed Fridthjof the Bold, whose saga was still told in many halls throughout the Northern lands, was an ambitious man who knew to take advantage of a situation when it presented itself.

One night, three years later, King Harald and his retinue were sitting at the feasting board in the royal palace at Geirstad when word came of long-ships sighted off the coast.

'You're certain they're not raiders bound for other shores?' King Harald asked the messenger. 'The waters off our coast is one of the busiest sea lanes in the area.'

Any ship sailing for the East Way must pass be-tween Agder and Jutland, south in Denmark. It was the king's exploitation of this strategic position that had made the southern kingdom powerful in the first place. But even after three years of recuperation, they were still undermanned.

'Nay, sire,' the messenger replied. 'They are sailing straight for Agder. And we've been hearing confused rumours of attacks on outlying villages in the west.'

With a bang, King Harald set down the boiled ham he had been gnawing on and rose to his feet. Queen Geirhild seized his ermine clad arm.

'What will you do, husband?' she said.

He shook his bearded head. 'We must send out the war arrow and prepare the kingdom for conflict.' He turned to his men, including his chief counsellor, the tall, thin, pale faced Mord. 'Mord, and you others. Come with me into the council chamber.'

'Aye, sire,' said Mord obsequiously.

The king seized a horn of mead and drank it down, then strode from the feasting board, with his chief warriors following.

Left alone, Queen Geirhild sat back at the high table and shivered despite the costly sables she wore over her slim shoulders. This was what came of setting her cap at a king. If she had married a farmer, she would have lived a peaceful life. Now she faced war and destruction as a yearly event.

'What's happening?' came a small but earnest voice.

Shocked, she swung round to see Vikar's tousle haired figure standing in the archway that led to their sleeping chamber, holding the hand of Starkad, now a boy of three winters, who was rubbing his eyes and yawning cavernously.

'What are you doing out of bed, both of you?' Queen Geirhild demanded. 'You should have been asleep hours ago.' What was the nurse doing, letting them roam around like this? She'd have the thrall girl whipped for her neglect.

Vikar dragged his unwilling foster brother with him to the dais. 'Is Father in danger?' he asked. 'We should go out there and fight the attackers.'

Starkad sat down wearily beside the fire trench, yawned, then curled up and went to sleep. Queen Geirhild climbed down from the dais, picked up the sleeping bairn and brushed the ash off his clothes. Without looking directly at her son, she told him, 'Your father is with his counsellors. He does not need a little boy's advice. Now take your foster brother and both of you go back to bed...'

She broke off at a sudden clamour from outside the hall. Steel rang, men cried out. Her husband could be heard in the yard giving orders. It seemed that the meeting in the council chamber had been rudely interrupted.

A single clang of iron resounded through the hall. Turning, she saw Vikar had gone to a wooden pillar and tried to take down a hand axe. He had dropped it in the process and that was what had alerted her. Now he tried to lift it.

'Stop that!' she called. 'What do you think you're doing?'

Angry, Vikar glared at her over his shoulder, straining futilely at the heavy weapon. 'I'm going to fight at my father's side!' he exclaimed.

In the queen's arms, Starkad gave a snore and snuggled more comfortably against her bosom.

'You are not!' she told Vikar firmly. 'Come here now!'

'I won't hide behind your skirts, mother,' the boy said. 'I...'

The doors burst open and in strode King Harald, flanked by men who were intent on the unseen situation outside, clutching at a sword wound in his right shoulder.

'What are these lads doing out of bed, woman?' he barked. 'Gather them up and prepare to flee!'

'What's happening out there?' she asked. The sound of fighting was growing louder.

'The men of Hordaland are attacking,' Mord murmured, clutching an unbloodied blade as the king opened a chest and took out bandages. 'They are already in the yard. They must have come ashore and marched inland in secret.'

'There's too much of this going on these days,' said the king, as he bound his wound. 'It's about time someone made himself king of all Norway. I've said as much before.' With Mord's help, he finished, then turned in the direction of the doors. He halted to point commandingly at Queen Geirhild. 'Take the children and hide them. Get away if you can. Take refuge in the Danish kingdom if we are defeated...'

The king broke off as a froth of blood flowed over his lips in mid order. Scrabbling at his back he turned to give Mord an unbelieving look, then fell facedown on the hall floor. The chief counsellor stood over his corpse, the blade in his shaking hand now bloody. He looked around at the warriors and the queen. Shrieking in horror Vikar returned to his struggles with the axe.

'We're surrendering,' Mord told the other hearth-men, who stared at him in bewilderment.

Two of them strode towards him, axes at the ready, beards bristling with vengeful wrath. But even as they did so, armoured figures issued through the doorway, weapons at the ready. Two of them cut down the axemen from behind. The rest of the dead king's hearth-men stood staring in horror as more Hordalanders entered the hall and took strategic positions, disarming the defenders as they did so.

Unspeaking, Mord stood over Harald's body. There was a pause, and then a tall, burly, bearded figure marched in. On his head was a glittering golden helmet. On his left arm was a brightly painted shield only a little battered by axe blows. In his hand he held an exquisitely worked sword, bloody to the hilt.

'Sire,' said Mord, bending his knee. 'As promised, I welcome you to a quiescent Agder.'

'My thanks,' said King Herthjof, flashing the queen a charming smile. 'And I see you have saved me the trouble of taking hostages.' He clicked his fingers. 'You! You, girl. Bring your brats over here. You all have a new master now.'

Queen Geirhild said naught, but stared in sick horror at her husband's body, the corpse of the man who had seemed so strong, so indomitable, and yet who had died in an instant, struck down from behind by a traitor. Vikar abandoned his struggles with the axe and ran wailing at Herthjof.

The king of Hordaland laughed uproariously, grabbed the small boy by his wrists in a ham-like hand, and hoisted him into the air.

'Here's a hell cat,' he boomed. 'With the right treatment, he'll grow up to be a fine warrior. A fine hater. For now, though, he'll be a hostage for the good conduct of his folk. As will his mother, and that idle lump in her arms.' He clicked his fingers. 'Take them away.'

He flung Vikar into the arms of a tall, one eyed man who wore a helmet with a long horsehair plume, who eagerly carried the boy out of the hall. Queen Geirhild allowed herself to be led, but she favoured Mord with a cold stare as she passed him.

In her arms, Starkad snored lightly.

2: Fenhring

THE BRINE STUNG Queen Geirhild's nostrils as spray drenched the deck. Starkad was demanding food. With Vikar following her, she left the wadmal tent where they had slept fitfully, and made her way up the swaying deck through the busy crewmen to the stern where the tall man stood at the sweep, single eye fixed on the distant horizon as the sun rose over the land. On either side, longships leapt the waves like a school of porpoises, sails cracking like whips in the bitter wind.

'I will need food for my bairn, man,' she told him. 'You! Yes, you. What is your name?'

The tall man turned to look at her and she quailed from that pitiless one-eyed gaze; like a solitary star glittering in unforgiving night skies. But it was morning now, and she knew that without food Starkad would suffer. So would Vikar. So would she, but she had to put her own needs last. She was a mother.

'The Hordalanders call me Grani Horsehair,' he replied. 'Have you no food for your bairn?'

'Nay, I have no food,' she said, flushing. 'And he is not my bairn. His mother is dead. There was a nurse who cared for him. I think she fled when your warriors attacked the hall.'

'Not my warriors,' Grani Horsehair told her. 'King Herthjof is master of this host.'

'Where is he?' she demanded. 'Will he talk sense? His servants do not.'

Vikar butted in like a young goat. 'Do what my mother says, old fellow.'

Grani Horsehair looked at him without speaking. Hungrily, Queen Geirhild found herself thinking. The wind moaned bitterly in the rigging.

The queen broke the silence.

'Don't speak like that to our host, Vikar. This man is our captor.' She turned to Grani. 'The bairn must be fed.'

'Oh indeed,' said Grani Horsehair. 'Fed, he shall be. He shall eat his fill, yet others must be content with their lot.' He looked back at Vikar. 'How did you become queen of Agder, lass?' he probed. 'You're not a woman of noble blood.'

The question distracted her from Starkad's wants. 'I… Folk say I am beautiful,' she managed at last. 'The king heard of my beauty and my skills with brewing ale, and rode to my father's steading.' She shrugged. 'He fell in love with me on seeing me and took me away to his palace.'

'It must have been difficult for you, dwelling in the royal household, a girl of common stock,' Grani said with unexpected sympathy. 'You would have had no knowledge of royal ways.'

'I should think not!' Queen Geirhild said with a bitter laugh. 'I had my rivals. I was not the only queen in Geirstad. Before me, King Harald married Signy, daughter of the king of Voss. They had not had children. She was understandably jealous on my arrival, and did everything to make my life hard. But I had friends, too. Powerful friends.'

'You must have done,' said Grani. 'Folk might say you had bewitched the king, a common girl like you winning his heart.'

Queen Geirhild gave him a startled glance. The steersman was strangely discerning.

'When I was a younger girl,' she said slowly, 'there was a man—oh, not like that! Don't stare at me that way! —no, it wasn't like that. I was dressing in my bower one morning when a man came to me. Gave me quite a fright, I assure you. I only ever knew him as Hood... He wore a hood always, you see. I never saw his face. He was a tall man, as tall as you.' She fell silent.

'And what went on between you and this hooded man?'

Geirhild flushed. 'Naught like that, as I told you! He said I could have aught I wanted,' she went on. 'I did not have to do aught, only call on him in all things. Well, that wasn't difficult, not when everything I called for came true. Then I told him, half in jest, that I wanted to be the queen of all the land. And it happened.'

'But the king already had a queen at his side.'

'Aye.' She nodded. 'I thought she might die and I would take her place, but it didn't work out like that. There we were, two queens in one palace. A man with two wives has twice the trouble, they say, and a kingdom with two queens is worse.'

'But you are now the sole queen of Agder. What happened?'

'King Harald decided to go a-warring that spring. He said that both his queens must brew ale, and he would keep she who brewed the best, that he would test it when he returned from fighting. I believe that Queen Signy was so desperate she prayed to the goddess Freya for aid!'

'And you?' That single glittering eye transfixed her. She licked dry lips.

'I called on Hood. He appeared in the brewhouse and spat on the yeast. He said that in return he would take that which lay between me and the brewing vat. There was naught there but empty air! I agreed, and when my lord returned victorious from the wars, I was pleased when he said that mine was the best beer.'

'And the price?'

She shrugged dismissively. 'As I said, there was naught between me and the vat but empty air. My lord was happy with me, and he put Signy away.' She smiled, and caressed the shoulders of Vikar, who was looking sullen, bored by all this grownup talk. 'Six months later I gave birth to a son, a successor for the king and my greatest joy.'

The ship bucked as the wind grew louder. Starkad started asking for food again.

Queen Geirhild tried again, shouting over the wind. 'He needs something to eat, we all do. You want him as a hostage, don't you? Then you must ensure he survives. Your lord king will not be happy if he dies due to your neglect.'

'Return to your berth, woman,' Grani Horsehair said, not looking at her. 'The fleet will weigh anchor at noon. Then we shall see if there is food to be had. None is aboard except stockfish, and that is not good for a growing lad.' He looked at her again. 'The king remains in Agder, levying a tax on your conquered folk. You and yours are hostages for their good behaviour. Agder will be part of the kingdom of the North Way. Your new lord will be the greatest king in the Northlands, until it is his time to cross the Rainbow Bridge.'

Another wave crashed down on the deck and he lifted his hood to shield his head from the spray.

Weary of the steersman's riddling speech, Queen Geirhild turned and scrambled with as much dignity as she could muster back across the deck towards the wadmal tent by the mast. Vikar came at her side, helping her keep her footing. He seemed more at home aboard the ship than her, walking with the same easy rolling gait as the crewmen who busied themselves about the deck.

But Grani Horsehair proved true to his word, and at noon they anchored off a half drowned skerry with the other longships. Grani sent men to the other vessels in search of food suitable for a lad of three winters, and at last a girl came bringing pulped grain in a small pot. To her surprise, it was the very nurse who had gone missing when the host of King Herthjof had descended upon Geirstad—she had been rounded up by the raiders along with other would-be escapees. Queen Geirhild had sharp words with the girl, but was grateful when she took Starkad from her care and fed him her pap.

Now the journey continued, and soon they were skirting the steep shores of Hordaland. They entered a fjord, mountain girdled, and the captives were brought ashore, most to be sold into thraldom. Queen Geirhild was taken to a well-guarded hall of the king's, built like a fortress with palisades and bastions and a dyke surrounding it, where she was kept as an honoured prisoner, her son Vikar with her. The nurse, and Starkad, were taken by Grani Horsehair to his home of Ask on the island of Fenhring.

'Why has he taken my foster brother away?' Vikar asked his mother the next day. He was missing his little playmate already. Besides, he couldn't see what made the boy important enough for Grani to take him away.

They sat in a curtained-off alcove of the hall, with a spear carrying sentry standing outside. Queen Geirhild took Vikar by the wrists and looked seriously into his eyes, saying, 'Listen to me, Vikar. We are at the mercy of the king and the king's men now. No one will be coming to help us. The king your father is dead, and his folk cannot rebel for fear of what will happen to us. I suppose that Grani Horsehair has taken Starkad away to split us up, to make it harder for us to escape, or to be rescued. He wanted to take you, you know!'

'Me?' said Vikar, eyes wide. 'Why me?'

She shook her head. 'I persuaded him to take Starkad in your place. It was a concession. Perhaps he found my ways winning! Should rebels come to rescue us, it is you who is of most importance. You are young, too young to fight, but they could use you as a figurehead...' She halted, frowning. He did not know what she was talking about. She wasn't sure she did either.

'The king killed my father,' Vikar said, seizing on something he could understand. 'I should kill him for that, shouldn't I? Just like in the old sagas.'

She shook her head, bit her lip. 'You're just a boy,' she told him sternly. 'You have no hope of revenge. You must accept your lot. If we please the king, persuade him that we do not intend to rebel, perhaps he will give us our freedom one day.'

Vikar shook his head vigorously. 'It is true what the man on the ship said,' he told her coldly. 'You are of common blood.'

Incensed, she struck the boy. He bore it without weeping.

'You will do as, as I tell you!' she told him, panting. Right now, she hated the horrible brat. He was more hateful than his father! 'You will be pleasant to the king when he returns from the wars. We both will. We will bow the knee to him and perhaps he will give us places in his kingdom. Do naught to anger him.'

Vikar opened his mouth in retort, but when she lifted her hand again, he thought better of it. But still, he did not bow his head.

The years passed, and on the island of Fenhring, Starkad grew like a young sapling, like one of the ash trees that grew in such profusion around Grani Horsehair's steading. It was a busy place in harvest time. In return for his services, King Herthjof had given his hearth-man fields and flocks and grain, and men to work the land. But Grani was seldom there, and young Starkad was often left to his own devices. It was a cold place despite its many fields, battered by sea winds on most nights, and Starkad, a quiet bairn, spent much of his time lazing by the fire in the kitchen house. In no way was he remarkable, except in his idleness—and his growth.

As soon as he was old enough no longer to need a nurse, the girl had been sold, and now there was no one left to remind him of his former life.

He heard news of the kingdom whenever passing traders stayed at the steading, or when his foster father returned from his warring in the king's name. King Herthjof's empire was growing rapidly, gobbling up many of the petty kingdoms of the south such as Jaederen and Hardanger, although he often needed to crush rebellions among the folk he conquered, and Grani had his work cut out fighting for the king. The only southern kingdoms to have escaped his wrath so far were Telemark and Upland, which were ruled by his brothers, although men whispered in secret that even here he was biding his time, building up his strength before he moved to strike.

Starkad yawned as his foster father related his most recent adventures, and poked idly at the fire as he lay before it. Grani Horsehair sat in his carved chair with its back in the shape of an eagle with ravens perching on its shoulders, its legs in the form of snarling wolves. He sipped a horn of mead, and said, 'Why don't you get up out of those filthy cinders, boy?'

Starkad looked up briefly and sighed. Grani Horsehair went on with his rebuke.

'You're growing up fast, lad, in height at least. But you spend every day lazing around the hall, the thralls tell me. One of these days you'll have to take some kind of action in your life, not lie in the cinders.'

'It's warm here,' Starkad said. 'I like to keep warm. And I like to lie here and think about things.'

'Dream, you mean,' said Grani Horsehair impatiently. 'There's more to life than dreams, boy. You'll amount to naught without deeds. One of these days, mark my words, you'll have to go to the wars.'

'Wars?' Starkad said. 'Fighting? But I might die.'

Grani looked at him long and speculatively. 'Oh no, lad,' he said at last. 'There's life in you yet. A long life ahead of you.'

'How can you say that?' Starkad asked. 'Are you

a seer? There was a spaewife who came last Yule-tide. She was a seer. But I can't imagine you can see much, with that one eye. How did you lose it?'

'It was the price I had to pay, long ago,' said his foster father, ignoring the boy's rudeness. 'You, too, will have your own debts to pay in life, you'll soon learn that. You'll have plenty of opportunity if the realm is invaded, which it may well be if the king continues his wars of conquest.

'A system of beacons is being established in the kingdom,' Grani Horsehair went on, 'to give advance warning of invasion by enemies, since the king is out of his kingdom so often, and the first beacon was built here on Fenhring. Your old foster brother Vikar has been sent to man it.'

Starkad had no memory of his childhood in Agder, and he took no interest in the news. Even hearing that Vikar had thrown his lot in with the king and joined his retinue did not trouble him. He had scant recollection of the older boy.

As his foster father droned on, Starkad lay by the fire, not troubling to avoid the ash and cinders which besmirched his ragged old clothes, one hand propping up his head while the other raked the embers with a stout twig, his lips twitching as he tried dreamily to compose a poem.

He stared into the fire, teased and taunted by visions conjured up by the flames. Or were they memories? Memories of fire and fighting. Memories of ice and ocean. Haunting memories like naught he had known in his present life. He didn't know where they came from. Perhaps they were memories of his earliest days. Or perhaps of another life.

3: The Beacon

THE BOAT CAME ashore on a rocky beach towards the north end of the island. In the distance, across the emerald waters of the fjord, dark grey smudged lines topped with green showed the location of adjacent islands. The water was cold as they splashed ashore, hauling the boat up behind them to a place above the high-water line. Once this was done, one of the four men from the boat, a stripling of about seventeen winters, climbed to the top of a grey cliff and looked around him.

Inland he saw woodland and moors. He wondered where the steading of Ask was to be found. He could see some farm buildings a little to the north west. Just as he was considering striking out across the moor, a shout from the beach caught his attention.

'Vikar!'

He turned, and the sea breeze caught his long fair hair, blowing it behind him like a king's banner. The same wind caught his dark blue cloak and it flapped around his shoulders like the wings of an eagle. His expression was an eagle's, too, cold and calculating. A faint fuzz of beard bleached his ruddy cheeks.

The tallest of the three men he had accompanied here was pointing up the beach in the opposite direction. They had finished stowing the boat, had loaded themselves down with supplies, and now were impatient to be off.

'The beacon!' the man added. 'This way!'

Without waiting for him, the three men turned and ploughed up the beach towards a headland where there were signs of new building. Recklessly Vikar galloped down the side of the cliff to join them as they reached the foot of the hill, where a gate stood in a palisade.

'Hurry up, lad,' said the tall man disapprovingly, his black beard caught by the same breeze. 'No time for dawdling. We've got a job to do here.'

'I know that, Sivard,' said Vikar. He sighed. 'It's so good to be out in the open air again.'

He had spent much of his upbringing a prisoner, in King Herthjof's fortress of a palace, with his mother. As she had wished, he had been cooperative with the king whenever he returned from his wars, and had soon won the man's trust. His mother had died of the bloody flux last winter, and now he was alone in the world except for King Herthjof's cronies. But he had not despaired. He had seen it as an opportunity. He had managed to win the king's trust so successfully he had been chosen to tend the beacon on Fenhring, first in the line of warning beacons leading from this outlying island to the palace at the head of the Byfjorden.

They reached the top of the craggy hillfort, where stood a tall construction of wood, a tower bearing on its top a platform for a fire. Stacked on every side of the tower were piles of brushwood, and several barrels of pitch were stowed beneath its cross timbers. A hut stood to one side, over-shadowed by the beacon.

A rickety wooden ladder led up to the plat-form up top, and it was only natural that the four of them should climb up there. Vikar came last, being the youngest of the men there, and he found his three companions gazing at the surrounding countryside as a bitter wind blew. Below them rolled the wide waters of the Byfjorden, its waves rising and falling as far as the horizon. Islands and skerries were visible on the eastern and western horizons, but northwards led towards the open sea.

A few fishing boats were visible in the fjord. At the heart of King Herthjof's growing empire, men could sometimes fish without fear of attack. There was that much to be said for his warring— he had brought peace, at least to Hordaland. But it was a fragile peace, often broken, and when any of the folk he had angered during his rise to power came looking for revenge, this was the way they sailed, through the tangled islands and into the great fjord at whose far end lay the king's fortified palace.

Vikar turned to look inland. Here he saw much the same vista that had met his eyes when he'd scaled the cliff by the beach, but here on the hill-fort, they were much higher up, and he could see further. Smoke drifted into the sky, indicating settlements some way south. He pointed them out.

'What are those places?' he asked Sivard.

The dark man grunted. 'Why, in the south east is the steading belonging to one of the king's most trusted hearth-men,' he told the stripling, 'Grani Horsehair. You've heard of him, lad, surely?'

'I think I have,' Vikar replied, not mentioning that he had been brought to Hordaland as a hostage by that very man. 'So, this is his island?'

'He owns a lot of land here,' agreed one of the other men. 'And elsewhere in the kingdom, too. But it's all under the management of stewards. He seldom sits quietly at home.'

'Always at the wars, isn't he?' said the last man, an elderly fellow with a missing hand. 'I remember him leading us into the fray in Jaederen, in the last battle I fought. But he'd disappear from the host for months on end. I never did know why.'

'Enough gossip,' said Sivard bleakly. 'We're here to do a job. The king trusts us enough to give us the first beacon to ward. From now on we'll be two men on, two men off. The first two will take turns to watch either direction. Meanwhile, the other two will sleep in the hut.'

'What about at night?' asked the elderly man.

'And do we have to stay in the hillfort all the time?' Vikar said.

Sivard looked at him with disfavour. 'Yes, you do, lad,' he said. 'The king's given you a job, and there'll be no time to go chasing the local women. I know what lads of your age are like. Believe it or not, I was young once.'

'Surely not,' said Vikar, straight-faced.

'For that, lad, you two can take the first guard,' said Sivard, indicating Vikar and the old man, who was called Karl. 'And yes, you will be watching until midnight.' He led the other man, Annar, down to the hut, leaving Vikar and Karl in the cold wind.

'Come on, lad,' said Karl kindly, leading him round to the seaward side of the platform. 'Seems the king thinks the warding of his lands of such meagre importance he leaves it to striplings and greybeards, but we'd best do our duty nonetheless.'

He hunkered down on the wooden platform and dangled his legs over the side. Vikar sat beside him, ignoring his sour smell, gazing out across the blue waters, scudded in places by white waves.

The wind never seemed to stop blowing, and it was a cold wind, for all that it was a west wind. It blew straight off the sea, and anyone would think it came from Jotunheim, those half legendary realms of frost where the giants were said to live. Soon Vikar's hands were frozen, despite the gloves he wore. Karl bore it all stoically, and began telling Vikar tales of his adventures in the warband of King Herthjof, before he lost his hand and grew old. Vikar was all ears at first, eager to hear any stories of warfare.

He had no real experience of the warrior's life, but wanted desperately to learn. It would surely prove useful someday. But after a while he found the old man repeating the same old stories in a sleepy drone, and he began to lose interest. He kept an eye on the empty firth, but as the sun set over the mainland his thoughts tended more towards the land. He felt an overwhelming urge to pay a visit to Grani Horsehair's steading.

But he resisted it and at midnight they were both relieved by Sivard and Annar, who took over for the next few hours. Karl and Vikar sought shelter in the hut, where a smoky fire burnt in the middle and they slept on beds of bracken. In the morning, they took over again, and stood on watch until noon. Sivard and Annar had naught to report. If any enemy ships had sneaked past in the night, they had done so without the lookouts noticing.

After another rest, Vikar was on watch that evening with Karl. The irregular sleeping was telling on the old man, and after half an hour, Vikar realised that Karl was snoring loudly. He glanced down towards the hut at the foot of the tower. Everything was still. Everyone in the hillfort was asleep except for him.

He rose to his feet and stretched. This watch was futile. The straits were dark, and silent except for a distant crashing of the waves. Although the moon was rising, he couldn't tell if any ships were passing in the night. Besides, what loyalty did he harbour for King Herthjof? The man had brought about his father's death at the hands of a traitor— Mord was now an important man in the burgeoning empire, one of Herthjof's counsellors—and then laid his native country under his tyrannical rule. Any Vikings raiding King Herthjof's kingdom were welcome to try their luck.

As quietly as he could, to avoid waking Karl, Vikar swarmed down the ladder. On tiptoes, he passed the hut where the other two slept. Then he hurried down the craggy slope to the palisade and swarmed nimbly over it, holding his sheathed sword in one hand and climbing with the other. Opening the gate would have been quicker but it would have made a noise that might have alerted the sleeping guards.

Now he was free. All that remained was for him to find Ask. The steading must be a league away or more. He'd better get going. It would take him all night.

He ran across the springy heather and vanished into the pinewoods with barely a sound. This area of the island was almost uninhabited, apart from occasional farms. At first, he felt exultant. He was free for the first time in years. In all his life. Before, he had always been someone's prisoner, at someone's beck and call. Even when he was a prince of Agder, in those long-ago days that he barely remembered, he had known naught that could be called freedom. Now it was just him, alone. Free. No one could tell him what to do now. He had no ties, no bonds. He thought he knew something of how Fenris Wolf would feel at Ragnarok, freed after an eternity in fetters.

As Vikar ran, he wondered what Sivard and the others would think when they knew he had gone. Word would get back to King Herthjof. He would forfeit the king's trust. Well, so be it.

But soon he was lost among the musty pines. He tried following animal trails, his feet almost silent as they padded across the drifts of needles, but the paths wound and twisted through the trees, never seeming to go the right way, which was south east. After a time, Vikar could no longer tell which direction he was going. Coming out into a small clearing he tried to get his bearings from the brilliant star field arching above, but soon gave up. He found a bush and crawled under it, wrapped himself in his cloak and slept until sunrise.

Now he rose, feeling hungry. He started walking with the rising sun on his left, keeping his eyes open for nuts and berries he could eat. After a quarter of an hour he breakfasted off a cloudberry bush that grew beside a limestone outcrop. This small feast gave him renewed energy for the rest of the journey.

He came out of the pines and found himself on the edge of some fields. He was weary, but he forced his pace until he saw a turf roofed farmhouse with a goat cropping the grass near the gable end. Brushing the pine needles out of his hair he did something about the travel stains his kirtle and breeks had suffered, then entered the garth. Asking directions of a stout, rosy cheeked woman getting water from a well, he followed a cart track towards the coast. It was midday before he reached Grani Horsehair's steading.

A thrall lazed in the sun outside the main farmhouse. When Vikar strode into the garth with all the confidence of a youth raised in a noble family, the thrall leapt to his feet, and grabbed his hoe as a free man might reach for a spear.

'The master's not here, wayfarer,' he said. 'Be on your way. Beg elsewhere.'

'Does your master know you greet guests so churlishly?' Vikar asked. 'Is this the hospitality Ask is so renowned for?'

The thrall lowered the hoe and leaned on it, scowling in puzzlement at Vikar, scratching his back with his free hand. He gestured idly at the doorway.

'You're welcome to come in, stranger,' he said grudgingly. 'Handcloths and a hearty welcome will be provided. But there's no one here but us thralls. And the lad, of course, but you'll get no sense out of him.'

'The lad?' Vikar echoed. 'I came here looking for a little boy. I suppose he must be twelve or so by now.'

The thrall shook his head. 'You must have come

to the wrong place, fellow. Looking at you now, you're no more than a lad yourself, but you've gone sadly astray if you're looking for your little playmate.'

'This is Ask? Grani Horsehair's steading? Grani's foster son is Starkad Storvirksson?'

'Aye, stranger,' said the thrall, puzzled. 'The lad's indoors.'

'You can announce me as Vikar Haraldsson,' Vikar said excitedly. 'Starkad is just who I've come looking for.'

The thrall gave him an odd look, but then he turned and led Vikar down the passage.

4: The Dreaming Hero

THE THRALL HALTED when he came out the other end of the passage into a gloomy room lit only by the glow of embers from the hearth. Vikar almost collided with him as he called out softly, 'Lad? Lad? Someone to see you. A guest.'

Something stirred in the shadows on the other side of the hearth. Something huge. Dry mouthed, Vikar edged round the thrall, as the latter tried again.

'Lad? Get up, can't you? Your foster father wants you to greet guests, you know. We don't get many as it is...'

There was a heavy sigh, like the snort of a horse. Vikar gagged at the reek that wafted out to him. It was so gloomy in here he really couldn't make out the figure that lay in the embers, but it certainly wasn't the little boy he remembered.

'Guest?' a dreamy voice drifted out. 'We don't get any...'

Vikar smiled at the thrall. 'I'll deal with this business,' he said. 'You can get back to work.'

Glaring, insulted, the thrall stomped back up the passage. Vikar turned and went to the hearth. He sat down on the ground and gazed silently across the guttering flames. In the embers on the far side lay a youth. A big youth. Bigger than Vikar. His head was propped in his right hand and in his left was a stick with which he poked idly at the embers.

'Is your name Starkad?' Vikar asked, feeling ill at ease.

There was a pause, then the big youth nodded slowly without lifting his head from his hand. 'Who... are... you?' As if asking the question was entirely too tiring, he yawned.

'Vikar Haraldsson,' Vikar said. 'I told the thrall to announce me. Vikar! Surely you remember me.'

'I have memories...' Starkad murmured. Vikar waited for more but Starkad lapsed into silence, peering into the hearth.

Vikar rose, and found a stool to sit on. He didn't feel at all comfortable on the ground, in the cold draught from the door, despite the heat from the fire. How Starkad could stand it, he didn't know. He must just have got used to lying in the embers.

'You were only young when the king's men came,' Vikar said. 'I doubt you remember much. I wasn't very old myself.' He paused and eyed the big youth dubiously. 'You've certainly grown since then! What are you, twelve winters old?'

'...Aye,' murmured Starkad.

'You could be just the fellow I'm looking for,' Vikar said. He paused. 'Do you remember what happened to your foster father?'

'Grani Horsehair? Why, he's away at the wars.'

Vikar shook his head. 'Before Grani fostered you, my father Harald was your foster father. King Herthjof had him murdered and took over his kingdom.'

He paused again, expecting some reaction. After a while, Starkad stirred. 'I remember... flames...'

'Ah!' said Vikar. 'That would be when you were very young. Raiders from Halogaland killed your own father. My father took you in and fostered you, brought you up alongside me. Then King Herthjof attacked the whole kingdom, and my father was murdered by his treacherous counsellor, Mord.'

He paused again. Starkad showed no reaction.

'Are you gutless, lad?' Vikar shouted, in a sudden outburst. 'Your father was killed, your foster father was killed, and all you do is stare into the fire! You should be ashamed. Get up!'

Impatient when the big youth still didn't move, he stormed round the hearth, his flapping cloak sending up clouds of smoke and embers. He seized the bewildered, protesting youth and hauled him remorselessly to his feet. It was like lifting a beached whale from the strand.

'...What are you doing?' Starkad was surprised to find himself standing on his own two feet. He lurched as if to fall, but Vikar seized him by his heft arms and held him up remorselessly. He peered into the youth's face. He was a head taller than him, and unless that was soot on the boy's face, he was already growing a beard. He stank like an ox.

Vikar let go and stepped back. Starkad clung onto a hall pillar and peered round him uncertainly. He shivered, and turned to sit back down at his fireside.

Vikar grabbed him by the wrist. 'No you don't,' he said. 'Stand up straight.' Starkad mumbled something. 'Speak up, boy!'

Starkad fell quiet. Vikar stepped back and examined him.

The big youth must have been all of six foot, if not taller. Curiously, Vikar used his hands to measure Starkad's huge arms. Then he inspected the youth's chin. Although both Starkad and his ragged clothes were covered in soot and ash, that was definitely a beard. Vikar patted ruefully at the fuzz on his own chin.

'You've grown,' he commented. 'Come out into daylight and let me look at you properly.'

In the garth, he met the thrall again. 'You've got him up off the floor!' the thrall said in wonder. 'Even the master couldn't manage that.'

Vikar shrugged. Starkad hulked over them, a woebegone expression on his face as they both peered at him.

'Those clothes are scandalous,' said Vikar curtly, indicating the grimy rags the youth wore. 'He needs a bath and a whole new wardrobe. This lad is the son of Storvirk, land warden of Agder, and he was fostered by King Harald himself. Why have you neglected him like this?'

The thrall shrugged, and scratched his back. 'Master tried to make him dress himself properly, but whatever he wore, he'd just lie round in the ashes all day. Those clothes were fine Irish linen when he got them. But he grew so fast and took no care over his appearance, and besides, the master is away so often...'

'Enough excuses,' said Vikar. 'Get a bath ready for him, and get him fine clothes and weapons. He's coming with me.'

A day later, Vikar and Starkad were in a small sloop, sailing away from the shore of Fenhring. In the distance, the steading was still visible. Starkad looked back longingly at the smoke rising from its roof as the wind whipped through the rigging and bellied the sail.

'I'm cold,' he announced.

Vikar looked up from the stern where he had taken charge of the sweep. It was an altered Starkad who stood on the deck. Still big—he might even have grown overnight, or was that the effect of his new clothes? —he stood up straight, and now wore a newly woven red kirtle over green breeks, and a green cloak hung down his broad back.

Washed and brushed, he was not unhandsome, and his long hair fell to his shoulders. A golden brooch studded with garnets clasped his cloak, and red gold arm rings like tail biting serpents wound round his forearms. Over his back, he wore a brightly painted round shield with a blue steel boss, an iridescent byrnie covered his huge chest, and at his side hung a well forged sword.

'You'll have to get used to the cold, lad,' Vikar said ruthlessly. 'We won't have much luxury over the next few years. We're warriors now.'

'Warriors,' said Starkad, as if the concept was a new one to this dreamy youth. He frowned. 'Who am I, Vikar?'

Vikar kept steering towards the rocky, tree lined shore on the far side of the fjord.

'You're Starkad Storvirksson,' he said. 'Didn't you know that much?'

Starkad shivered again. 'Sometimes, in my dreams,' he murmured, 'I think I'm someone else. I'm pacing across endless ice fields. I'm going to meet my intended. I never do.'

Vikar scowled. 'You should dream less and do more. We're outlaws now, lad, rebels against the kingdom of Herthjof. We've got no time for dreaming, only achieving.'

'Outlaws?' the lad said. 'Rebels?'

Vikar nodded. 'We've disobeyed the king's commands, stolen his property. Now we're going to fight him.'

Starkad's dreamy eyes focused for a second on Vikar.

'Who's the dreamer now?' he said. 'I know what war is like. I know two boys can't fight a kingdom.'

'What do you know of war?' Vikar asked. 'Nay, don't tell me—you know it from your dreams,' he added, as Starkad began to describe the battles of trolls and giants. 'Aye, I know we're too few to declare war on Herthjof,' he added. 'But there are others who are discontent with his rule. Herthjof has made himself many enemies. And those enemies are the ones we will recruit.'

Starkad's clouded eyes were clearing. 'You've been planning this for a long time,' he said.

Vikar nodded his head. 'I have,' he acknowledged. 'You're not the only one who's spent his days as a hostage in dreams, but mine weren't of legends and the past, mine were of the future.'

Starkad flushed angrily. 'They're not just stories,' he said. 'My dreams are real. Real memories. I was a giant once.'

'You're no dwarf now,' Vikar commented sardonically.

Starkad shook his head. 'Who was he, foster brother? That man I am in my dreams? That giant who fought other giants?'

He cringed involuntarily at a rumble of thunder from above the distant hills.

'I remember stories I heard as a boy,' Vikar said thoughtfully. 'It was said that your father was of the blood of trolls. My mother told me not to repeat the tales, but folk whispered that your grandfather was of the blood of the giants, and your grandmother a princess from the world of the elves. Foolish tales, no doubt.'

Starkad rubbed at his face. 'Grani Horsehair told me naught of this,' he said. 'Just told me to get up out of the ashes and do something with my life. But as long as I remember I've wanted to do naught but sleep and dream.'

'You were more lively when last I knew you,' said Vikar, eyes on the nearing shore. 'It seems we both were altered by our suffering. I bent the knee to the man who had my father murdered. That was my mother's counsel. I had no chance of vengeance when I was a mere stripling. But now, you and I, we're men. Even if you're only twelve winters old, you're full grown and strong nevertheless. And I know that together we can gather a band of outlaws and berserks who will fight for us and help us gain vengeance and a kingdom.'

They came ashore. Securing the stolen boat to a birch that overhung the water, they scrambled up the bank and made their way through a meadow and into the dark eaves of a pinewood.

Soon the ground began to slope upwards, and Starkad found the going troublesome, though his legs were longer than Vikar's. The avenue of boles led away into musty murk, like the pillars of an enormous hall, the sort he remembered from his dreams, a hall of the giants. He felt small, though it only took a glance at the older youth beside him to realise he wasn't. But his great feet made no sound as they paced across the needle strewn floor.

A dead quiet hung over this place. At times, he caught a distant croaking of birds from beyond the roof of branches. Otherwise there was no sound except the cracking and thrumming of twigs as they pushed their way through the more overgrown stretches. These were few. Otherwise the aisled hall of pines went on and on, up and down needle swathed outcrops, but trending ever upwards.

'Can't we rest?' Starkad asked, his thighs aching as they came out into a green clearing between stands of pines. 'Where are we going? Are we still in Herthjof's kingdom?'

'He certainly lays claim to these forests,' Vikar said, pausing to look in exasperation at his companion. 'You can't be tired, surely. We've not gone half a league.'

'Is that all?' Starkad said, although it sounded a long way to him. 'I've not been out for a while. What do you mean, he lays claim to them?'

Vikar sat down, and unslung the pack he had been carrying. As he tugged at the drawstring opening, he added, 'There are others who claim these forests as their own ground.'

'Oh,' said the big youth in a small voice. He sat down, leaning against a bole, and watched an industrious swarm of ants carrying pine needles to a nearby anthill. This was starting to seem like hard work. 'I'm hungry, too,' he added.

Vikar had opened the pack and now he flung the youth a lump of stockfish. 'I thought you would be,' he said, producing another, and starting to gnaw on it.

Starkad copied him unenthusiastically. He

didn't like stockfish unless smeared with butter, and he doubted his foster brother had brought any. What did he mean, others?

'Do you mean outlaws?' he said eventually. 'Where do they live?'

'I don't know,' said Vikar. 'We could be searching for days. They don't advertise their presence. But it is said that outlaws dwell within these forests.'

'And you want to recruit them?' Starkad said. 'Won't they just rob us?' He shook his head. 'All this consorting with rogues and thieves. I can see you swinging from the gallows one day, foster brother.'

'Maybe,' said Vikar laconically. 'Feeling afraid?'

Starkad didn't know how he felt. He was sure that he had fought worse opponents than outlaws and robbers in his life. He was only a boy of twelve, and yet he knew that he had been a warrior, a hero. But when? Was this some kind of memory of his grandfather's life? Did his veins run with the blood of trolls and elves?

As long as it didn't end up running on the dry earth of the pinewood.

'Are there wolves in these forests?' he asked, still watching the busy ants. His own life seemed aimless in comparison, for all this notion of a quest for vengeance.

Vikar nodded, 'I should think so,' he said, 'and bears.' He drew the drawstring of his pack and climbed back to his feet. 'Not afraid, are you?'

Starkad shook his head. 'Look,' Vikar went on, 'I've been a prisoner and a hostage as long as you. I don't know the forests any better than you do. But I do know that we won't be able to regain our kingdom and avenge my father unless we find folk to help us.'

'What if these outlaws don't want to help us?' Starkad asked. 'What if they just want to kill us and rob us?'

'There's no answer to that,' Vikar said. 'Come on.'

Starkad rose and together they entered the trees on the other side of the clearing.

They were making their way up a narrow defile shortly after when Starkad heard stealthy movement from the trees on either side. Glancing up, he saw a dark silhouette leap into cover behind a thicket. More noise came from ahead, more dark shapes seeking cover. Vikar halted.

'What now?' Starkad whispered.

'I think the outlaws have found us,' Vikar whispered back. 'Time to see if they're willing to help us.'

Starkad heard a crash behind him. He swung round and saw a man charging down the bank towards him, the deadly looking axe in his hand glittering strangely in the eerie forest light.

5: Thirteen Warriors

S TARKAD DREW HIS sword and swung it, splitting the man's skull to the teeth.

He spun round, sword crimsoned, to see two or three more men plunging down from the thickets.

Vikar looked wide eyed at Starkad, nodded at the corpse at his feet, and said, 'Good work, foster brother.' He turned to face the other outlaws who were coming down the defile in a raged crescent.

'We've killed one of you already,' Vikar said, raising his voice. 'We're not here to fight...'

A tall, gnarled-faced, black bearded man came at him with a wickedly sharp spear. Vikar caught it in his shield, then lunged in low with his sword. Letting go of his spear, the man leapt back. Vikar flung the shield, now too heavy to hold, down to the mud, and gripped his sword firmly. The man drew his own sword and came forward with it extended. Starkad pushed past Vikar and engaged the man.

He had never fought before but as he forced the man back with swashing blows, it all seemed to come to him so easily. He was blooded now, and there was no turning back, no second retreat into dreams. Somewhere in the back of his mind, the battle was neverending. It had begun before he was born and would last until long after his life-span was measured. He felt the shock of metal on metal as their blades clashed again and again.

To his right, a man leapt down to engage Vikar. Sparks flew in the gloom as blade rang on blade.

Starkad stormed forwards, sending Black Beard staggering back over a tree root as he came on in a whirl of steel. The outlaw scrambled to his feet again and Starkad's sword swooped like a hawk. Blood showered the mud. Starkad stepped over the twitching corpse to face the last man stand-ing, now Vikar had despatched his own attacker. The survivor wore the masked helmet of a chief-tain, and through the eyeholes he looked on in sur-prise.

But he faced the two warriors bravely, looking from one to the other, brandishing his sword and beckoning. 'Would you attack me together, like cowards?' he boomed from beneath his ornately worked helm. 'Or would you duel with me; to the winner the spoils?'

Starkad stalked forwards. He had discovered he had a thirst for slaughter. But Vikar seized his arm and halted him. Starkad's foster brother looked around at the corpse littered defile, appalled.

'We didn't come into these forests to fight,' he began.'

'How can I believe you?' the helmeted man thundered. 'When you have slain all my fellow outlaws? You were tracking us down to our hideout. Now you've killed my men, but I'll take you both with me to board with Odin.'

Starkad threw off Vikar's restraining hand. 'Let me kill this fool,' he growled.

Vikar looked at him in wonder, then shook his head. He turned back to the helmeted man.

'We came looking for you, aye,' he told him. 'But with a proposition. I'm seeking men to help me regain the kingdom that is mine by right. Will you join me?'

The man turned to look at the fallen. He wrested the helmet from his head. 'You leave me with little choice,' said the pale eyed man with a braided beard who was revealed. 'If you slay so many when you are recruiting, you'll have none left to take on your enemies.'

Starkad snatched up some grass and wiped the blood from his blade. He sat on a rock, produced a whetstone, and began to hone his blade. Vikar introduced them to the man, who was called Hildigrim. He had been living in the forests ever since King Herthjof's men had burnt his village in a punitive raid against rebels in the region. The rebels had already moved on, but new rebels were created when the survivors took to the woods and to killing the king's men whenever they met them. Now Hildigrim was the last survivor, but he was all the more willing to join Vikar's small warband now he knew his aim.

He laughed uproariously. 'We three against the most powerful king in the Northern lands? By

Odin, it's a tale for the skalds.'

'There are very few of us,' Starkad agreed. 'Grani Horsehair says that King Herthjof's ships are so many a man can walk from Agder to Jutland by leaping from deck to deck.'

Vikar shrugged dismissively, as if this was a small thing.

They helped Hildigrim bury his former comrades. 'I was not a kinsman of any of these men,' the outlaw said. 'Besides, they had prices on their heads. They were any man's to kill.'

But Starkad was wary of the man. Was this just a bargain of necessity?

'Do you know of any other men who might be ready to fight against King Herthjof's tyranny?' Vikar asked as they followed Hildigrim back to his lair among the rocks.

'A league to the west dwell the sons of Herbrand,' Hildigrim said. 'They have lived like trolls since they were driven out of the kingdom after their father was outlawed for robbing travellers. Their father died in a raid on an outlying steading, but they have kept up his ways ever since. They are not good men,' He shook his head thoughtfully. 'But they will join any insurrection, if there is plunder.'

'How many men?' Vikar asked.

'Herbrand had nine sons, but one is no more,' said Hildigrim. 'I shall call them tomorrow.'

The following afternoon, Hildigrim's rocky lair was crowded. All eight of Herbrand's sons had come, tall, grey eyed men with dark hair, clad in ragged clothes and weighed down with spears and axes. Their leaders were Ulf, a swarthy man, broad across the shoulders and as tall as Starkad, and Erp, his scrawny, vicious brother. The others were Sorkvir, Grettir, An, Skuma, Hroi and Hrotti. Starkad distrusted them all, but Vikar welcomed the brothers with the gentility of a born prince.

'And this is your war-host, lad, is it?' said Ulf, his eyes darting like gnats in a beam of forest sunlight. 'With this host, you'll seize the kingdom?'

'Better you join your robber band with ours,' Erp counselled Vikar, 'and we'll live by preying on the weak as we always have done.'

Vikar shook his head. 'We need a few more men,' he said, 'and then we will strike. I have a plan.'

'Tell us,' said Erp, with a look of weaselly cunning.

'Not yet,' said Vikar. 'How do I know I can trust you?'

'I say you can't.' Starkad spoke frankly. 'These are robbers, not trusty warriors.'

Ulf came over to him and peered menacingly into his face. 'Who is this over lofty fellow?' he growled.

'This is Starkad Storvirksson,' Vikar said, 'who was fostered alongside me in the palace of my father, Harald of Agder.'

Ulf turned again. 'You really have a claim to a kingdom? I thought you just a mooncalf lad with big dreams.'

'I am the true heir to the kingdom of Agder,' Vikar informed them all. 'What is more, I spent many years in the hall of King Herthjof, and I know every nook and cranny.'

Ulf and Erp exchanged glances. The other brothers rumbled appreciatively.

As the new recruits fell to a meal of stockfish and ale, Starkad took his foster brother to one side.

'How do you know we can trust these thieves and sons of whores?' he asked. 'You'll gain no honour associating with the likes of them.'

'You've become wise in the ways of the world very quickly, for a dreamer,' said Vikar in some annoyance. 'Where else will we find support? Vikings will not give us credence, and besides, they would want to see gold before they agreed to fight for us, even if all we're left of the spoils is not enough to fill a cat's nostril!'

'You have some plan?' Starkad said.

Vikar nodded. 'I've been planning all this for some time, as you know.'

Starkad glowered down at him. 'What is your plan? Tell me!'

Vikar smiled thinly. 'I think I'll keep that to myself,' he replied.

Starkad gestured at the hungry robbers as they sat wolfing down their stockfish. 'You trust these strangers more than your own foster brother.'

Vikar put his hand on Starkad's arm and gazed at him.

'I trust you, foster brother,' he said. 'It's not that I think you'll betray me to King Herthjof. But I don't want to commit myself to a plan. It may need to be changed, as circumstances change.'

'I don't think you really have a plan,' Starkad said at last.

'Starkad! You—and our followers—will learn my plan at the right time. Now go and eat. Try to make yourself popular with our new friends.'

Starkad went to get himself some stockfish from the stores, but he sat on his own, and as he ate he cast suspicious glances at the newcomers.

'I appreciate you want to keep your plans to yourself,' Hildigrim told Vikar respectfully. 'But surely, we will need more men than this to seize a kingdom, by Odin.'

Vikar drained his horn goblet of ale before speaking. 'We will need more men,' he acknowledged. 'I do not intend to move at once. Besides, the king is away at the wars. Which gives us time to gather such forces as we require.'

'I know of two duellists,' said Erp. 'Styr and Steinthor, brothers, from Stad in the north. They wander the land making trouble for farmers, fighting and bullying for title to men's property. They're not got what they're looking for yet.' He nodded. 'They'd join us.'

Starkad sighed irritably. Vikar gave him a quelling glance.

'They sound like fine fellows,' he said. 'where will we find them.'

Erp looked evasive. 'They could take some tracking down,' he said. 'I'll guide you.'

'My thanks,' said Vikar, as grandly as the king he hoped to become.

For a second time Starkad took him to one side.

'Let me come as well,' he urged. 'This robber will betray you.'

'But I need you here,' said Vikar. 'Someone's got to keep an eye on the others. You can train them for the coming fight while I'm away.'

Starkad nodded seriously. 'I'll soon have these curs whipped into shape,' the twelve-year-old assured his foster brother.

'Good man,' said Vikar, reaching up to slap him on the back. 'I knew I could depend on you.'

Leaving Starkad in charge of the training, Vikar set out with Erp on the trail of Styr and Steinthor. The journey took them along some of the less frequented byways and seaways of King Herthjof's kingdom. Along the way, they fell in with travellers who shared news and gossip of the kingdom. Vikar learnt that his absence from the beacon on Fenhring had not gone unnoticed, and he had been outlawed in his absence, becoming a wolf's-head like Erp and the others, to be killed on sight.

Learning this, he kept away from settlements as much as he could, but it was still necessary to venture into inhabited areas to learn news of the duellists. In a trading centre on the coast they heard word of two men terrorising remote farms up in the hills, men with a price on their heads. They turned inland and on stolen ponies ventured into wooded valleys on the edge of the icy mountains.

One morning as they were riding up a valley, they heard a girl's scream ring out. Vikar and Erp exchanged glances. Erp kicked his pony into a gallop and shot off, followed by Vikar. Turning a corner, they came out of the forest and rode out into a river meadow. A farmhouse stood beneath the mountainside, and in its garth a confrontation was taking place.

Two scruffy men, clad in skins and furs and holding bearded axes, stood within the pale. Facing them was a farmer, and in the porch of the hall stood two women, a stout matron and a girl of marriageable age, who was crying. As Vikar and his companion rode up, the men's voices became audible.

'...hand over your fields and flocks and we'll let you go unharmed,' one of the axemen was saying. 'Otherwise you must fight us for them. We're notorious duellists know the length of the North Way. You may have heard of us—Styr and Steinthor, from Stad in the north.'

'Be off with you,' the farmer said in a quavering voice. 'We don't want your sort round here.'

'If you're difficult, we could make things difficult for you,' the other added. 'That's a pretty daughter you've got. We could get a good price for her at market. She'll be a little... shop-worn by then, of course.' The girl sobbed.

The man broke off as Vikar leapt the pale on

his pony and halted beside them. Erp followed circumspectly. The farmer and his family eyed Vikar warily, while the two duellists veered round to keep these newcomers in sight.

'What d'you want?' the first duellist demanded. 'Find your own steading.'

'Styr!' cried Erp. 'My lord here is the rightful king of Agder. He's looking for men to help him win back his kingdom. Interested?'

A week later, they all rode back into the camp among the rocks to find the robbers training enthusiastically under Starkad's eye. Despite the tall youth's lack of experience, he somehow knew exactly how to transform them into a fighting unit.

Starkad broke away from his charges as he saw Vikar and the others ride in. 'You found them, then?' he asked.

Vikar nodded. 'Starkad, this is Styr, and Steinthor.' He turned to the two fur clad duellists. 'This is my foster brother and right-hand man, Starkad.'

Hildigrim came up to join them. 'Twelve men against a kingdom, now,' he commented.

'Do you know of anyone else who would fight for us?' Vikar asked. 'My plan needs only a thirteenth warrior.'

Hildigrim and Erp exchanged glances. 'Gunnolf Blaze,' they both said.

But word must have got out, because the following morning, the far famed berserk and outlaw strode into the camp, having passed the sentries without them seeing him.

'Who's in charge here?' demanded the tall, fair haired, long bearded man in the wolf skin cloak. He saw Hildigrim and greeted him as an old friend.

Vikar stepped forward. 'I'm in command,' he said. 'Who are you?'

'This is Gunnolf Blaze,' said Hildigrim. 'Seems news travels faster than Odin's ravens these days.'

'An old man told me you were hoping to topple this tyrant king,' said Gunnolf Blaze. 'I have no love for him since he destroyed my Viking fleet some years back.'

Vikar studied the newcomer, noting the blaze of white in the man's forelock. 'I've heard of you,' he said. 'They say you are a fine fighter and a good general. You may well find yourself in charge of the war-host of a king.'

Gunnolf Blaze looked around darkly. 'I see naught but a nest of robbers,' he said, 'though you have the eyes of a lad with king's blood in your veins. Your war-host is elsewhere?'

Vikar shook his head proudly. 'This is it,' he said. 'With this band, I intend to take on a kingdom.'

'I thought you said a war-host,' Gunnolf Blaze muttered. 'Pity. If you had a war-host, this would be the right time to rise. King Herthjof's fleet has been seen coming up the Byfjorden. He's back from the wars, loaded with plunder, his men weary after months of hard fighting.'

Again, he looked round at Vikar's pitiful handful of thieves and outlaws, and he shook his head.

6: The Hall Of Herthjof

A DAY LATER found them hacking their way through thick fir woods that overlooked the fjord where King Herthjof's palace was found. Eleven men forced their way through the vegetation while the rest kept watch. They were nearing the king's farms now, and it was inconceivable that sentinels were not patrolling these woods. Over the ridge behind them was a sheltered bay where they had moored the small longship, provided by Gunnolf Blaze, after sailing here from their hideaway out in the islands. Starkad felt exultation course through his veins as they came out into broader, well-kept woodlands. The ground was sloping downwards now, with rocky outcrops on either hand, and he knew that after an hour or two more of travel they would be looking down from the eaves of the forest at the meadows surrounding the fortified palace of the king.

'The dreamer has awoken, eh?' said Vikar, marching at his side. 'Time we took our vengeance, foster brother.'

Starkad glanced over his shoulder at the rabble of robbers and outlaws coming after them. He had licked them into a fighting force, he knew it, but where they were going there would be hundreds of men confronting them. King Herthjof ruled over most of Southern Norway, and his retinue was huge. The only advantage they had was the fact that Herthjof's men were back from the wars, weary and wounded, many of them. But they had been victorious, so their morale would be high. An attack by thirteen warriors, thirteen outlaws out of the forests, would be a small thing to such a host.

They reached an area surrounded by outcrops, a natural amphitheatre among the trees and rocks, and Vikar called a halt.

'Starkad, take two men and scout out the approach,' he said. 'I want to know how ready the enemy is for attack.'

Starkad nodded. 'And the fortifications?'

Vikar smiled. 'I know enough about them,' he said. 'Don't forget, I spent many years as a hostage in that palace. I know all its ins and outs.'

Starkad nodded grimly, gestured to Hroi and Hrotti, two of Herbrand's sons, and led them out of the bowl of rock and down a narrow track through the trees. Ravens croaked in the welkin above, following them as they crept downhill. Starkad gave them a baleful look. Soon they would be descending in flocks to feast upon the fallen. But whose fallen?

'Look!' hissed Hroi.

Making their way through the trees just below them were four men in armour. Guards of King

Herthjof. 'We must be close,' Starkad murmured, but even as he did, a man in a glistening byrnie glanced idly uphill and his mouth dropped open.

'Robbers!' he shouted. 'Kill them!'

The men turned, spears lowered, to confront Starkad and his two men. Starkad knew he had the advantage of higher ground, and surprise, but it wouldn't last.

'Agder!' he shouted as a battle cry, and threw himself down on the man in the byrnie. Hroi and Hrotti surged past and engaged the two men behind him in a clash of steel that rang back from the surrounding timber, while the last of the guards stood in the rear, spear poised, waiting for a chance on this narrow hill path to get a thrust in at the attackers.

Starkad dodged a sword slash from his opponent, kicked out with a big booted foot and bashed the man's shield back into his chest, overbalancing him. Not waiting for him to recover he hacked with his sword, cutting deep into the man's neck. Half decapitated, the guard fell.

At the same time, Hroi speared his foe and the man hit the dirt, eyes staring, face stilling into the rictus of death. Laughing as his own attacker turned to run, Hrotti cut him down. Even as he did so, the last guard fled helter-skelter down the wooded hillside.

Starkad grabbed a fallen spear and flung it javelin-like after the vanishing figure, but it sank deep into a tree bole while the guard disappeared out of sight.

'He'll be off to warn his king.' Starkad cursed. 'After him!'

They ran down the hill, dodging between trees as the wood thinned out. At last they came to a halt at the edge of the wood as it opened up into meadows, fenced with hurdles. Sheep and cattle cropped the lush sward, tended by thralls. In the distance, surrounded by palisades and moats, dominating the head of a fjord thronged with fleets of longships, was the massive hall of King Herthjof.

Running through the gate into the garth was the distant figure of the fleeing guard.

Starkad cursed again. 'Now the king will be ready for us,' he said. 'We'd better get back to Vikar.'

Angry, he stomped up the wooded slope, Hroi and Hrotti trailing after him. They passed the corpses of the other guards, already buzzing with flies while ravens lined the branches above. But the birds made no move towards the bodies. It was as if they were expecting a feast of which this would be a mere appetiser.

'Got away?' Vikar demanded when Starkad and the other scouts reported to him. 'You should have slain him.' He ignored Starkad's snarl and turned to the others, who were sitting on fallen logs. 'Time to move in! They're ready for us, so be prepared.'

They reached the edge of the wood without further incident, and strode down the grassy hill with ravens flocking above them. The thralls Starkad had seen were hastily herding the cattle and sheep in through the massive gates as warriors shouted at them and urged them to hurry.

'Now!' yelled Vikar. 'Agder! Agder! For my father!'

The thirteen warriors pelted down the grassy slope and over the fields as the herds vanished inside the stockade. Warriors peered down from the ramparts. Vikar flung his spear at their leader and he vanished out of sight with a cry, spear jutting from his mailed breast. The rest of the guards withdrew into the garth.

'Do they run from a dozen men?' Starkad laughed.

'I fear a ruse,' said Gunnolf Blaze thoughtfully. 'How do we get through those gates? They'll be waiting inside in ambush even if we do.'

Vikar led them along the bank of the dyke to a place at the far side from the great gates. 'I learnt of this way out when I was a hostage,' he said, grinning. 'I doubt those guards know what a boy brought up here knows. Half of them aren't even Hordalanders.'

He lowered himself into the dyke, felt about with his feet, and then stood up, the water pooling round his thighs. 'A hidden causeway,' he said, leading them across it. 'An escape route in times of attack, I suppose.'

They reached the other bank without incident.

As Starkad examined the palisade, a shout came from a tower along the way and then the ramparts were lined with spearmen.

'Up the walls and at them,' Vikar said, scrambling up the side of the palisade following a path of almost indiscernible notches. Starkad followed close behind. As Vikar flung a leg over the spiked top of the palisade, spearmen came running. He drew his sword and rushed to meet them. In seconds, Starkad was at his side.

Together, they fended off the spearmen. Starkad got past the guard of one, and flung him over the side into the spreading waters of the dyke, narrowly missing Gunnolf Blaze who was still scrambling up the side. Vikar parried a spear thrust, hacked off the spearhead and then sank his blade into the man's neck, between byrnie and helmet. As the man fell off the parapet another came forward and lunged, his spear bouncing off Starkad's byrnie and pinning his cloak to the palisade. Vikar was trapped in the middle, between the spear and the palisade, and he jabbed at the man with his blood slicked sword, but his opponent knocked his blade back with his shield, almost pushing him over the side.

Now Gunnolf Blaze joined the fight, smashing the man's spear with his axe and kicking him backwards so he collided with a man coming up a pole ladder from the garth below. Starkad saw the garth filling with men flooding from the large, ornately gabled hall on the far side. Shouting 'Agder!'

he leapt from the parapet into the midst of them, cutting several down with his sword as he shot down meteor-like among them. Vikar and the others leapt down to join him. They had slain several men before a horn note belled out across the compound and the survivors fought a rear-guard action, vanishing into the hall through its great gates.

Starkad looked around to see only his fellow warriors on their feet. The fallen spearmen of King Herthjof littered the ground. Ravens lined the gables and shingles of the hall.

'So, these are the conquerors of Norway,' he crowed. 'Running like rabbits into the safety of their hall!'

Vikar joined him. 'I hoped they wouldn't do that,' he said. 'That place is virtually impregnable.'

'I once knew a girl like that,' said Erp, hovering at his elbow. 'She was big with bairn six months after meeting me, all the same.' He produced a fire steel. 'Shall we burn the place down? With them in it? Tried and trusted.'

Vikar shook his head firmly. 'I want to meet my enemy face to face, steel in hand.'

'Aye,' said Hildigrim with a wolfish laugh. 'We'll go to Odin with sword in hand.'

'You dwelt here for years, foster brother,' said Starkad, tired of the banter, 'while I lazed by Grani Horsehair's hearth. Surely you know a way into the hall.'

Vikar shook his head. 'I had hoped to encourage Herthjof to come out and meet us,' he explained. 'Now he's in there...'

Starkad saw a tree trunk lying in the entrance to a workshop. A sawyer had been at work on it, lopping its branches for some rebuilding work.

'Follow me,' he told the warriors.

Carrying the trunk between them as a battering ram, they hurried towards the great gates. These were nine feet high, surrounded by wooden ornamentation in the form of gripping beasts and serpentine knotwork. Figures in the form of the stags that devour the leaves of the world tree were carved into them. They were locked fast. From within came a hubbub of conversation.

'Come out, king of Hordaland,' Vikar bellowed, 'or are you too craven to meet your match?'

There was no reply. Gunnolf Blaze looked sharply at Vikar.

'Seems you have your answer,' he said. He shifted his grip on the battering ram. 'You're doing better than I expected,' he admitted grudgingly. 'For a dozen and one warriors to have sent King Herthjof's men scuttling into their hall, that's an achievement—unless it's all a trap. But can you do better?'

'Yes, I can,' said Vikar. 'We'll smash down those gates and rush the hall. King Herthjof will die here today, or surrender on his knees.' His eyes narrowed. 'And there's another I wish to find. Mord, my father's treacherous chief counsellor. If I find him, only one of us will walk away.'

Starkad wondered if Grani Horsehair was within. What would he say if he met his foster father on the field of battle?

They charged the doors and the battering ram thumped them so the carvings shuddered and shook, and a dent appeared in it, but they were not broken down. They stepped backwards for another charge. This time, as the ram pounded into the carved wood, a split appeared, but even as it did, steaming hot oil poured down from the eaves above them, narrowly missing the warriors.

'Back!' shouted Vikar, and they hurried away out of range.

'Again!' Vikar insisted. 'We're almost there, lads. Good work! One more try.'

They sped across the garth, even faster than before, and the ram smashed into the doors, shaking them so hard that one of them seemed to open for a moment, but the locks and bolts held. As more hot oil poured down, its threat augmented by a shower of arrows from concealed slits, they sprinted back again.

'One more try!' Vikar egged them on.

They ran across the steaming ground, which had been turned muddy and greasy by the rain of hot oil. Erp slipped and lost hold of the ram, but the rest crashed into the doors with it, breaking them open with a slam and a resounding crack. Erp scrambled back to his feet, plastered in mud, and ran to take his position with the others as they poured into the hall beyond.

The great open space rang to the cruck beams with the din of blade on blade as the warriors of King Herthjof set upon them. Starkad found himself fighting six or seven men. It was like confronting a wall of steel and hatred as the byrnie clad, helmeted warriors attacked. Starkad's sword darted here and there as he swung it like a sickle, reaping an awful harvest of blood and brains and tripe and guts. He split skulls to the teeth, lopped off limbs, thrust his sword into hearts and hacked off heads. All around him his comrades were at the same horrific work. Soon the floor of the hall became a shambles of gore and red meat and pooling, stinking snakes of innards, that had once been the warriors of King Herthjof.

But of the king there was no sign.

At last they forced the wall of men back to a point halfway across the floor of the great hall. Hungry ravens had entered through the gates and now they lined the hall beams as expectantly as they had the limbs of the trees in the forest. The beams themselves were inlaid with red gold and studded with gemstones. Bright banners swung from the rafters in the rising heat from torches that shed a red light over a sea of blood that covered half the floor and lapped at the fire trenches.

At last Starkad could see the dais on the far side, beneath a carving of writhing dragons. Standing there, dwarfed by the immensity of the hall, on the far side of a sea of helmets that represented the warriors still to be fought, stood a burly, grizzle bearded figure wearing a golden helmet. At his side was a tall, thin, pale faced man in black. And on the other side was a man who wore a helmet with a horsehair plume, wrapped in a cloak of dark blue. Starkad recognised the latter as Grani Horsehair. It could have been his imagination, but he thought his foster father looked thoughtfully from him to Vikar and back again, although the one-eyed man's expression was unreadable.

Vikar pointed with his bloody sword at the man in the golden helmet. 'That's the king! That's Herthjof!'

Starkad stepped out in front of the still standing enemy warriors. He gestured at the blood-stained floor behind him. 'Must this slaughter continue? Or will the craven king who hides behind his men face me in single combat?'

Silence was his only answer. 'Well?' he said impatiently. 'What is it to be?'

7: King Of The North Way

GAIN, GRANI HORSEHAIR seemed to look on from the dais, but this time Starkad imagined a hint of disapproval. While he waited for an answer from the king, Starkad thought about the events that had brought him to this point.

King Herthjof rose, cast his cloak from his shoulders, drew his sword and flung away the scabbard, then strode with shield on arm through the ranks of his spearmen to where Starkad stood. On his face was a resolute expression, but as he strode he glanced back at Grani Horsehair. Grani's face was implacable.

The king halted a yard in front of Starkad.

'What makes you so eager to smash and destroy what other men have built up?' he asked in ringing tones. 'It is I and no one else who has welded together the petty, squabbling kingdoms of this land, each tucked away in their separate fjords, each preying upon the other. I have built an empire, such as the Greeks have, such as the Danes had under Frith-Frodi. I have built the mighty kingdom that was prophesised of old. And you, you robbers from the woods, wish to drag it down, to shatter it, to reduce the lands of the North Way into the chaos that we knew not so long ago. What makes you so eager, tall man?'

Starkad was tongue tied. Never had he thought of King Herthjof as aught other than a bloody handed killer, a tyrant, an enemy. Now he could see that uniting the kingdoms of the North Way was a noble enterprise. And yet...

'You killed my foster father,' he choked. 'You took me hostage and made my folk your thralls!'

The king shrugged. 'Some will always be thralls,' he reasoned. 'The weak enslave themselves. To the strong belong all things.'

'Then we shall test who of us is strongest,' said Starkad. 'If you live and I die, why, then, to you belongs your empire. But if I am victor, then my lord, Vikar son of Harald the Agder king, will take your realm.'

The king flexed his muscles, brandished his sword. 'But what's in it for you?' he said, his voice a murmur that no one else heard in that high, echoing hall, not even the ravens that crowded the cruck beams overhead, seemingly intent on their every word. 'You allow yourself to be led like a sheep when you have the heart of a wolf. A lone wolf. Why should you fight for another? Or, if you must, fight for the strongest, not this leader of forest outlaws.'

Starkad struck with the swiftness of a snake. The king brought his glittering blade up and the clash of steel rang out clear and harsh in the expectant hush of the hall. Starkad faced the king, who had moved slow but mighty, like an ox, as he crossed the floor, but now seemed as fast as a hardened man of war. He probed with his sword and Starkad knocked it back with a circular parry. The king feinted low and Starkad brought his blade down, but then he jumped back as the king's sword whipped at his throat.

'A cunning king,' Starkad panted.

'I didn't become king of the North Way by being a fool,' King Herthjof replied, as they circled each other, blades glittering in the firelight. 'Nor will your lord. I know you now, Starkad the Idle, who lay in the ashes by Grani Horsehair's hearth. Get back to your fireside, boy; this fight isn't for you.'

'In this existence, I was a lazy lad who lay by the hearth until my foster brother woke me to my duty,' Starkad acknowledged, 'but in another life, I was a slayer of men and a ravisher of women that only a god could kill.'

'I've heard of that Starkad,' said the king. 'May Thor guide my stroke and may I live to tear the limbs from your overlarge trunk!'

On the last word, he struck.

Starkad leapt back deftly, but he stumbled, and the king was upon him again, surging forward. Yet Starkad's stagger was feigned, and even as the king came at him, he dodged to one side, then brought his sword round in a scything circle and almost hacked off Herthjof's outstretched sword hand.

The king scrambled back, panting. He laughed harshly.

'Is this Vikar's champion?' he asked. 'You are naught, a mere green, untested boy, for all your freakish lankiness. Why does Vikar not fight his own battles?'

'Harald of Agder was my foster father before Grani Horsehair ever took that role,' said Starkad furiously. 'This fight is mine.'

'A fight you seem unable to win,' the king sneered. He shouted at Vikar. 'Come, king's son!' he invited. 'Will you not fight at your champion's side? Seems he cannot kill me alone.'

Starkad spat. 'Do not shame me so,' he snarled as Vikar strode forwards. 'I will kill this tyrant...'

He leapt back suddenly as the king cut at him with his sword.

'If you fought like a man,' Vikar cried, 'and not a sneaking coward, then my champion would cut you down like tares amid wheat. But since you leap and claw like trapped vermin, very well! We both shall bait you.'

Proudly, the king drew himself up, looking from one to the other, his eyes grey and cold, his beard bristling, his helmet glimmering in the torchlight.

'Come one, come all,' he said. 'I'll fight you both and slay you both. It will be to my honour and your shame. I am king; you are naught but robbers and outlaws.' He gestured to his men, 'But let me not hold you back, warriors of Hordaland. While I settle this small matter, you may chastise these other wolf's heads.'

At this invitation, Herthjof's surviving men marched forwards, flowing round the three fighters in the middle of the hall, and set upon the remaining half score of rebels.

Starkad glowered resentfully at his king. 'This is my fight, foster brother.'

Vikar ignored him and swung his sword at the king, who deflected it with his shield, then spun on his heel to meet the attack of Starkad.

Herthjof grinned humourlessly. 'For all your words, you'd take advantage, eh?' he spat. He darted forward and pricked Starkad's cheek with the point of his sword.

Wrathful, Starkad swung up his sword in a wild parry, knocking back the king's blade. Even as he did, Vikar thrust at Herthjof round the rim of his shield and hacked deeply at his shoulder.

The king, eyes wide, dropped his sword and clapped a hand over the deep wound. Vikar stepped back. 'First blood to me, I think,' he said.

'Not true,' gasped the king, as Starkad allowed him to snatch his sword from the floor. 'I blooded your lofty friend first.'

'Not just a friend,' Starkad snarled. 'I am his foster brother. What's mine is his, what's his is mine. And your life is mine.'

But even as he spoke, Vikar's sword swept down. Crimson blood sprayed the churned-up ground, and the king fell lifeless.

A score and a half of men fell with Herthjof that day, but Vikar's forces sustained no losses. Vikar clasped his foster brother to his bosom beside the corpse of King Herthjof, but ever after their comradeship was colder. Starkad never forgot how his foster brother had taken from him the kill that was his by right.

At last, Mord came forward, accompanied by Grani Horsehair, who had accepted defeat amicably to Starkad's surprise and relief.

'We accept you as our lord,' Grani told Vikar. 'These forces are now yours to command. All the fleets and warriors of the king who you slew.'

Mord, however, looked less sanguine. He stared in horror at the king's blood laced carcase.

'Grani, and all these men will I accept,' said Vikar. 'But this man'—he pointed at Mord— 'is a murderer, and will be treated as such.'

Mord fell, sobbing piteously, at Vikar's feet. Vikar kicked him aside like a cur, and turned to Starkad.

'Hang him from the gables outside.'

The assassin's body still hung from the rooftree, picked over by ravens and kites who had gorged themselves all week, when Vikar set sail upon the fjord in Herthjof's flagship. No one paid the cadaver any heed; all were intent on their mission, to secure the empire of Herthjof before it fell apart into petty kingdoms again, each fjord and bay and mountain ruled by a different king or earl.

Starkad lounged in the stern with Vikar, resplendent in the golden helmet of Herthjof and a deep red cloak, as Grani Horsehair stood at the sweep.

'And what when you rule Herthjof's empire?' Starkad asked his foster brother. 'This began as a quest for vengeance. It has become something greater...'

'A quest for glory,' Vikar said. 'It was Harald King of Agder's dream—my father's, your foster father's—to unite the kingdoms of the North Way. We shall fulfil his dream, beginning with the work that our fallen foe began. Agder shall be liberated, Hordaland and Hardanger and Jaederen shall come beneath my sway...'

'And then?' asked Starkad. 'Will you sail north into Halogaland? It was from that country that my own father's killers came, you said.'

Vikar smiled thinly. 'The Far North may need to be pacified some day,' he admitted, 'but there is no profit in those barren lands. No, I hope to set my sights on another quarter. The East Way shall see the sails of the fleet of Agder and Hordaland.'

Starkad looked out to sea, and made no comment.

'Wherever you go,' said Grani Horsehair from the sweep, 'men will flock to your banner. But will you unite all the kingdoms of the North Way? Only Skuld, youngest of the Norns, knows what is to come. Would that it could be revealed to others.'

'No man can know his fate,' said Vikar, 'but at least we can live as warriors, and die as befits men —fighting our foes.'

'Such will not be your weird, king of the North Way,' Grani Horsehair assured him, and as he spoke, Starkad saw something in the glint of his foster father's single eye that he did not like.

As they sailed on up the fjord towards the open sea it was not the cold breeze that made him shiver.

STARKAD THE TRAITOR

1: King Of The Rus

O N THE SHORES of a vast lake, two armies faced each other in silence.

This was not their native land. Both were foreign armies, meeting in a land they did not know. The wooded countryside of the Gauts flanked them on one side, on the other the waters of Lake Vanern reflected their glittering ranks. One army, from its pony tailed helmets and its elaborately embroidered tunics of white or cream, baggy trousers and kite shields, hailed from across the tideless East Way, in Gardariki, the half mythical land of the Rus. The other, from its round, painted shields, its sarks of blue mail, its helmets of black iron with eye and nose protectors, and its bearded axemen, could come only from one or other of the kingdoms of the North Way, Hordaland perhaps, or Agder.

Indeed, the second war host bore the green tree banners of the king of Agder, whose longships had won him an empire that united the disparate sea coast tribes and kingdoms of that land of fells and fjords. It was an empire built on that of Herthjof of Hordaland, who had conquered the kingdom of Agder, ruled by the father of Vikar—the tall, keen eyed young warrior standing beneath the great

fluttering banner at the centre of the line, surrounded by burly, bearded warriors. Now Vikar
had avenged his father's death at the conqueror's
hand and gone on not only to seize his empire
and to expand it. Now his conquering army had
reached as far as Gautland, where Odin's grandson
King Gautrek was lord, but it was not the Gauts
who his war host had met, but a foreign army.

'We are the warriors of Sisar of Kaenugarth!'
cried the gaily clad popinjay who was the enemy's
herald. 'Our keels brought us to this western land
where we have plundered and slaughtered. Our
wagon trains are heavy with the loot of the Njars
and the Gauts. None have dared withstand us.
Who are you who block our path? Be gone, before
we slay you also.'

A big man stepped forward from Vikar's army,
one of his twelve elite warriors, a youth by the
look of him, though the truth was he was younger
even than his seeming years. Yet a long beard jut-
ted from his chin, and his stalwart thews were
those of a grown man. In one hand, he held a longsword, in his hand a shield emblazoned with the
same green tree image as that on the banner of the
war host.

This was Starkad, foster brother of Vikar and his
greatest champion. 'My lord king Vikar is ruler of
all the lands of the North Way,' Starkad told the
popinjay. 'All the fjords and fells and islands bend
the knee and pay tribute. Only in the north and
the east is his rule yet to be felt. But a foreign army,

from the luxurious lands of the East, is not welcome here.'

'We shall not give ground, tall man who speaks for this dunghill cock called Vikar,' the Rus herald called back. 'We are here to take what is ours. And what is ours is what we take. Run home to your kennels, tails between your legs, dogs of the western lands. We Rus live not in a land of luxury as you deem, but in a country of ice and snow, a land that breeds men.'

Starkad turned to King Vikar and spoke to him in an undertone. Then he turned back to the herald.

'Ready yourselves for war, foreign thieves and robbers,' he cried out, 'for the men of the North will not give ground, rather we shall take it!'

As he stepped back into the small group surrounding Vikar, the king gave a sign with his hand and a horn blower put his horn to his lips. A series of notes belled out and the Northmen archers nocked arrows and bent bows. Even as they did, the Rus herald scrambled back to his king's retinue.

Arrows swooped across the field, first from Vikar's side, then from Sisar's, darkening the sky they were so many. Arrows sank into the turf, into painted linden shields, into byrnies, into flesh. Screams tore the air, men fell to the turf. The lines of warriors on either side were broken, like a comb that lacks teeth. But still many hundreds stood, shield in hand, spears glittering.

Vikar turned to Starkad. 'Now is the time to wash our spears in blood.'

He gave the order to the horn blower and more blasts rang out. But even as they did, the ranks of the Rus advanced. Spears dipped to thrust out like hedgehog spines and the turf thundered to the running feet of the raiders.

'Charge! Charge!' Starkad bellowed, forcing men forwards with blows. He brandished his sword as he ran. 'Agder!' he bellowed. 'Agder!'

The air was alive with tension as the two forces ran headlong towards each other, as if a thunderstorm was brewing. But cloudless blue dawn skies arced over the field as the racing armies were mirrored in the spreading waters of Lake Vanern. Starkad ran at his king's side. Vikar always led from the front, unlike some kings who preferred to direct their wars from the safety of their men's midst.

'Form a wedge,' Vikar shouted, and he and his thirteen champions formed into a V-shape with Vikar at the point, Starkad on one side and the hardened, grizzled warrior Gunnolf Blaze on the other. Ahead of them the Rus troops were advancing at the run. Remorseless, helmeted faces peered over shield rims, spear points levelled.

Then the two armies met in the middle of the field, and a great clag rang out from the nearby timber. Shield thumped into shield, both lines shivered with the impact like a tree in a storm, but stood firm. Starkad found himself face to face with a crazy eyed Rus man, helmetless, with a head shaven but for two scalp locks beside his ears. He wielded a large axe one handed, a formidable weapon as Starkad found when it hammered a slice out of his shield.

He was a big fellow, but Starkad was bigger, and when another axe blow lodged in Starkad's shield, the Northman warrior plunged his sword into the Rus man's unprotected face so it sank in halfway to the haft. The dead Rus fell back, almost snatching the sword from Starkad's hand. The warrior next to him, an ill-favoured man with a fur trimmed helmet, lunged at Starkad's now unprotected neck.

At the last moment, Vikar was there between them, his sword glittering the morning sunlight as it sliced through the Rus' arm. The severed forearm and sword fell to the turf in a spray of blood. The Rus stood there gazing stupidly at the gushing stump of his arm, then fell helplessly after them.

'My thanks,' said Starkad, then flung himself at his king, who staggered back as two Rus rushed up, spears levelled, but missed Vikar. Starkad swung his sword in a web of steel, successfully cutting down one warrior, but the other man sank his spear deep in Starkad's thigh. Gritting his teeth against the pain, Starkad hacked down with his sword, breaking the spear haft with a crack, then brought his sword arcing back up again to split the man's chin with the tip.

Grunting, Starkad sheathed his sword and

wrenched the spearhead from his thigh. Blood reddened his breeches but still he strode on into the melee.

The fighting was at its thickest around Vikar and his champions. Sorkvir and Grettir fought back to back, Steinthor on the ground with an arrow through his arm. Styr was fighting a broad-shouldered, fur clad, fair haired man whose armour was gilded and who wore a circlet on his helmet. In one hand he wielded a sword and in the other a thrusting spear, while over his back was a small shield with a pointed boss. On either side of him were squat, swart faced warriors who fought with scimitars.

Even as Starkad watched, the fur clad man cut Styr down.

Starkad strode to confront the man, standing over Styr's fallen form. 'Who are you, man?' he bellowed, 'so Starkad Storverksson can add your name to the tally of his dead?'

'Arrogant pup!' roared the Rus warrior as his swart companions fended off Northman attacks. 'It is Starverk Storkadsson whose name will be remembered as one of the many who fell before the sword of Sisar, fighting king of Kaenugarth.'

Starkad swung his sword at Sisar, and the man blocked it with his elaborately ornamented sword. He traded great ringing blows with this man, leader of the Rus war host, and the dust of the battle field swirled around them as they fought. Sparks rained down as steel collided with steel.

Sweat ran down into Starkad's eyes.

He brought his shield up to meet a swing from King Sisar but the impact of the blow knocked it from his hand. Starkad brought his sword up but too late as the Rus king's blade sank into his scalp. Now blood joined the sweat in his eyes and he staggered, stars exploding in his sight as Sisar rained blows down on him, cutting open his left cheek, then ploughing down into his collarbone.

While Starkad was still staggering under the storm of blows, the king brought his sword round as if he was beating an errant child, plunging it into the Northman's side. Even as Starkad was trying to bring up his sword the Rus thrust his spear deep into Starkad's other flank.

Starkad dashed the blood from his eyes. He swung his sword round, cutting deep into Sisar of Kaenugarth's side. Then with all his power he swung the weapon at the king's leg below his knee, sinking in deeply. Sisar staggered. Starkad swung the sword again at the other leg, and cut off the man's foot at the ankle. Sisar fell like a mighty tree brought down by a storm.

He looked around him, weak from his wounds, to see the battle still boiling about them. But new forces had appeared, Northmen like Vikar's army but with different emblems on their shields and banners, showing crossed arrows. For the moment, they stood in the eaves of the forest, watching the fight down by the shore in uncertainty.

Starkad reached down and sawed busily for a

moment at the body beneath him. At last he knelt down then rose bearing the severed head of Sisar. He found Vikar.

'I've killed their king,' he said. 'They're still fighting.'

'Not for long!' said Vikar. 'Get a spear!'

When Starkad shortly afterwards lifted the head, still dripping gore, above the embattled warriors, a hush slowly descended on the field. One by one, men on the Rus side faltered and began to move away. Chieftains and champions among the Rus tried to stem the tide, but soon there was a steady flow of fugitives running back the way they had come, along the path between the lake and the forest.

It was now that the men Starkad had seen earlier issued forth from the woods, attacking the fleeing Rus, cutting them down, or shooting them down with arrows or throwing spears. As they poured down from the forest, Vikar's men attacked the few steadfast Rus, and even these broke and ran.

Starkad did not join the rout. He lowered the spear that held the severed head of Sisar and leant upon it, head bowed as blood dripped from his wounds. He felt dizzy.

He came to himself to hear Vikar speaking.

'...and this is my greatest champion Starkad. See? He has been wounded many times and yet still he stands.'

Starkad glanced up, and almost fell. Vikar, who

was standing before him with a short, dark haired man with keen eyes in his broad face, leaned over and steadied him.

'We need a leech,' he observed.

'I'll see that one is found at once,' said the dark man, and he made a sign to another warrior whose shield was emblazoned with the crossed arrows emblem. The warrior returned shortly after with a sober looking man in the grab of a healer, who searched Starkad's wounds.

'This is Olaf, king of the Njars,' said Vikar, as Starkad bore the leech's ministrations with fortitude. 'His realm suffered defeat by the Rus, and his sister was borne off as a captive, along with many of his people.'

'But thanks to your intercession,' Olaf said approvingly, 'my people are avenged, the captives freed. We pursued the Rus back to their camp and slew them, plundering their possessions, many of which were ours heretofore. Thank you, Starkad Storverksson. Like your liege, you have done the Njars a great service today.'

Starkad grunted wordlessly. He knew little of the Njars, other than that their land was one of the petty kingdoms of the Swedes, lying to the east of Lake Vanern, and that an early king, Nidud, had taken prisoner the famous smith Volund. He also noted that they had waited until it was clear that Vikar's side had the upper hand before they had leant theirs. But he tactfully forbore from making this observation.

It seemed that they had won an ally in these parts. Despite some misgivings, Starkad felt that Olaf might prove useful.

2: Herthjof's Brother

HIGH UP IN the mountains, a kingdom had established itself amid the fells and dales. Further east, the land was locked in snow and ice, and no one lived there but for robbers who infested the forest paths that led across the range of mountains known as the Keel and down into the Swedish petty kingdoms. But in the fertile dales of the Uplands were many hill farms and settlements, and their ruler was Geirthjof, one of the three Grandsons of Fridthjof the Bold. Until the rise of Vikar, the three Grandsons had ruled all the surrounding kingdoms; Geirthjof ruling the Uplands, Herthjof ruling Hordaland and Agder and adjacent lands, and Fridthjof, eldest grandson of Fridthjof, ruling Telemark. When Geirthjof received word of Herthjof slain, he was perturbed.

'By rights I should seek vengeance,' he growled to his men. 'And so I shall. But my elder brother Fridthjof is absent on a Viking raid, and it will be a pity to go against this upstart from Agder with only half our forces.' He peered out at his huscarls and earls from beneath shaggy brows, hoping for encouraging words.

'Better that you go with your own retinue and their war bands,' said tall Grim, stroking his long beard with one hand and gesturing to the huskarls with the other. 'Then when your brother returns, he will find you king of the Uplands and of Horda-land and the folk of the fjords.'

Geirthjof grinned suddenly. 'Fridthjof won't like that,' he said. 'I will rule all the lands that our forefathers took under their sway bar Telemark, and be the most powerful king of the North Way. What's more, no longer will I be pent up in this landlocked mountain kingdom that my brothers left me, but I will have access to the fjords and the sea, and able to go plundering on Viking cruises at will, without having to pass back and forth through my brothers' dominions.'

For a moment, he allowed his bushy moustache to droop. 'I mourn Herthjof's passing,' the king assured them. 'But I shall avenge it mercilessly. The skalds will sing of the slaughter I wreak until the Doom of the Gods. Who is this Vikar? I have never heard of him.'

'They say he is a young man,' Grim murmured, looking to his comrades for confirmation. 'Son of the former king of Agder, who was slain by your brother. Vikar was taken hostage for his people's good behaviour, along with many other noble youths. He proved himself loyal in his new lord's eyes and was set to guard the seaward approaches.

'But he escaped with his fellow hostage Starkad and together they raised a rabble army that some-how overthrew your brother's host, accepted those who surrendered as warriors of his own, and went on to consolidate its grip on the lands he formerly ruled. But now he has gone eastward to plunder in the Swedish kingdoms, and his realm lies open to attack.'

'Then despatch the war arrow to the outlying shires at once,' Geirthjof commanded. 'We shall gather the greatest army the Uplands have ever known, and descend upon the fjords and farms of this upstart with fire and the sword. When he returns, he will find his stolen kingdom a wasteland. And when my brother Fridthjof returns from his cruising, he will show more respect than he has been of late.'

As messengers set out from the garth of the king's dwelling to raise the war host of the Uplands, Geirthjof took Grim to one side and they spoke under four eyes in an alcove curtained off from the main hall.

'You say my brother's men now march with the rebel Vikar,' he said. 'Can any of these be contacted? If we can persuade them to see where their true allegiance lies, they may turn against the usurper and aid us in our own fight.'

Grim looked thoughtful. 'There is the man Grani Horsehair,' he said cunningly. 'He was one of your brother's right hand men. You may remember him. I know how we could contact him and sound him out...'

Shortly after his return to his farm on Fenhring, Grani was approached by agents of the king of the Uplands.

He had accompanied Starkad and the king of Agder and the other lands on their raid into Gautland. It had been his honour to give tactical advice during their advance from the Vik and around the shores of the great Lake Vanern, biggest of the lakes of the Northlands. A greybeard as he was, he had not joined them on the field of battle.

Some whispered that he had no real loyalty to the new ruler of the former empire of Herthjof, but why should they think that? Very well, he had once been a hearth-man of the former king, Herthjof, but he had also become foster father of Starkad, Vikar's foremost friend and right-hand man, after Harald Agder-king was slain. And the bond between foster son and foster father was famously stronger even than that between father and son. Perhaps that was why he had gone over to Vikar's side.

But when a small group of warriors from the mountains called at his farm, he did not mention his bond with Starkad. The lad was at court in Agder, leagues from here, with his king, celebrating their victory over Sisar. And these mountain men spoke little of such matters.

'You swore oaths to King Herthjof,' their long-bearded leader blustered, standing over Grani as he sat in his elaborately carved wooden chair, 'to serve him unto the death. Not to outlive him. And yet you turned your coat and granted your favours to the usurper, when you saw which way the wind was blowing.'

'Which way the wind blew,' Grani murmured. 'Indeed, that is true.'

'But you know where your loyalty lies,' the bearded man went on, hectoringly. 'The usurper is in a bad position, between we folk of the fells on the one hand and the people of Telemark, whose ruler was also a brother of Herthjof. Both kings are obliged to avenge their much-loved brother. It will be short shrift for traitors when they invade these stolen lands.'

'I hear that Fridthjof of Telemark is at the wars,' Grani said. 'Do you mean he will return with his hosts?'

'Word will reach him,' the leader assured him. 'And he will return vowing vengeance. Two great kingdoms against the usurper...'

'You have heard that Vikar gained a victory in the east?' Grani said. 'And returned laden with plunder, and with new allies in those lands?'

The bearded man crouched down by Grani's chair.

'You're no fool, old man,' he said. 'You know that such victories mean naught. Conquest is all that matters. And the surviving grandsons of Fridthjof the Bold will conquer this kingdom. The lot of traitors is terrible. I warn you. As a friend, I warn you. Think where your loyalty lies, old man.'

'I see that clearly,' said Grani in a quiet voice.

The bearded man shook his hand while the other guests from the mountains muttered their approval. 'Well done, sir,' Long Beard praised him. 'Then you will do as we suggest?'

'Speak, man,' said Grani, 'and I will listen.'

Word came to Vikar in his hall in Agder of hosts massing in the mountains. He called a council of war to which came his hearth-men and closest confidants.

Starkad was first to speak.

'Sire!' he said darkly, 'we must strike first! This Geirthjof has vengeance on his mind—aye, and conquest. It is the blood feud that motivates him chiefly...'

'His brother slew my father,' Vikar began, but Starkad interrupted—the only man at court who would dare.

'And perhaps your father slew his father, and all the way back to the first killing, when Odin and his brothers slew the first Frost Giant. But these Grandsons of Fridthjof have ambitions beyond their family honour. They dream of ruling all the lands of the North Way.'

'As does any Northman king in his right mind,' Vikar replied. He clenched his fist and pounded his ribcage. 'But it is I who will rule over all the petty kingdoms!'

Starkad relented, and nodded. 'In which case, we must be first to strike.'

'I know a way we may bring this war to a swift conclusion,' said Grani Horsehair from his place amongst the other counsellors.

Starkad swung round to look closely at his foster father. 'Tell us,' he urged. 'You have never failed the king yet with your redes.'

Grani Horsehair went to the trestle table on the side of the echoing hall, and indicated that they should all gather round. Hastily he gathered together plates and platters, drinking horns and goblets.

'Here is our position, on the coast,' he said, taking a hunk of bread to mark Vikar's hall. 'Here'— he placed several goblets in a line— 'is the Keel, the high mountain ranges between our lands and those of the Swedish kingdoms. North of here is the Dovrefjell, the troll-haunted mountains that divide these lands from Halogaland and the north. Down here, in these dales'—he marked them with a string of sausages— 'are the Uplands. Here will Geirthjof gather his forces, at the meeting point of these rivers.' He pointed them out. 'If we can forge a way through this pass, we will be able to attack his host from the rear, when he is least anticipating it…'

'But this will leave us open,' Vikar pointed out, 'from the mountains. As we try to flank him, we will leave my domain open to attack. What if his host is faster than us?'

'Even more reason to make haste, before King Geirthjof has time to muster his forces,' Grani Horsehair said with a cunning grin.

Slowly, Vikar nodded. He could see no fault with the plan as such. But he didn't like the look of those valleys. The whole kingdom of the Uplands could so easily turn into a death trap.

As soon as Vikar had raised his own levies through his kingdoms, the host set out up the dales and into the mountains. Starkad marched at the king's side, the rest of his champions going with them. Ahead went trusted Agder scouts, riding on ponies as they quested in search of defenders. Behind came the earls of Agder and Hordaland and Vikar's other realms, men of the sea coast in their helmets and byrnies, marching up and up into the half barren mountains.

The air grew colder as they went, the skies above the azure hue of the icy skull of Ymir from which the gods had built the heavens, the forests on either hand dark and musty, the streams swollen by ice melt racing down the valley bottom. But soon they left the beaten tracks of the Upland marches and were travelling through the side valleys where few but herdsmen dwelt, where glaciers flowed not rivers.

Nights they spent shivering with cold, bundled up to each other, eating hard tack and stock fish, not lighting fires for warmth or cooking. Vikar lost several men this way, but he was undeterred. Losses were inevitable, Starkad knew, but he hoped it would not be his own weird to die that way, miserably, of cold.

He had been healed of his wounds, to the wonder of all. Most men would have died of any one of them, but he had spent a short time abed and risen refreshed and healed. His dreams had troubled him during his period of recuperation, and he had remembered times long gone, memories of a life other than his own. It haunted him, and reminded him of his youth when Grani Horsehair fostered him.

Starkad was troubled, also, by his foster father himself. The man marched along with them, but he said little. He had, after all, served Herthjof before he joined Vikar's rebel army. Now he was Vikar's foremost strategist. But could he be trusted? Starkad was his foster son, and even he did not feel he truly knew who Grani was. The man vanished at strange times, to return unlooked-for.

And true to type, one morning he was missing.

'Where has he gone?' Vikar demanded. 'You, Starkad. Don't shake your head like that. You know him, he's your foster father. Where has Grani Horsehair gone?'

Starkad spread out his arms.

'I cannot say, sire,' he informed his king as they stood together in the centre of the barren valley as the sun rose and the camp came to life on every hand. 'He will be back, that is all I can say.'

'Back?' said Vikar. 'Back from where? With whom?' He looked warily about him. 'Your foster father has betrayed us, Starkad.'

'I can't believe that, sire,' Starkad protested, but there was little conviction in his words.

'What do we do now, sire?' asked Grettir, looking nervously about him. The misty crags lowered down at them from the cliff faces, as if the mountain giants frozen into stone by daylight were looking down in disapproval at the lost army. 'Do we retreat? Return to Agder?'

'Nay,' said Vikar, shaking his head. 'If we go back, we will have lost valuable time. We go on.'

'But, sire...' said Grettir. 'If Grani is a traitor...'

The king would not listen. He forced a march up the bleak, lonely valley.

Fog rolled down from the barren crags. With uncanny speed, the dale was buried beneath it, and the warriors were marching blind through cold, wet mist. Starkad spoke again to his king.

'Sire, we must turn back.'

'I'd never thought Starkad Storverksson would counsel retreat,' said Vikar sardonically.

'You know I have sworn never to retreat from fire or iron,' said Starkad, 'like the rest of your champions. But this is not an army that faces us. It is the weather. The fog. We cannot go on under these conditions. Even if this mist is not of sorcerous work, we could march over a cliff at any moment. We do not know where we are going.' He stopped in his tracks, but Vikar stomped onwards.

Starkad hurried after him. 'At least call a halt until the fog lifts.'

Vikar would not listen to him. Cursing to himself, Starkad followed his liege. On every hand, he could hear marching feet and jingling armour. Strange echoes magnified it until it seemed to be coming from all directions. Was it Vikar's war host? Those dark shapes moving in the mist, were they Hordaland and Agder fighters?

Grettir joined him, and Sorkvir. 'Where does the king lead us?' Grettir asked. 'We are lost.'

'It was your foster father who suggested this route,' said Sorkvir accusingly. 'Where is he now? He has betrayed us!'

'Say no word against my foster father,' Starkad growled. 'And I'll hear no griping at the king, either!' But inside, he was troubled.

The noises in the mist grew until it sounded like an army was tracking them through the fog-shrouded valley. Men began to mutter amongst themselves. Starkad spoke sternly to them, appealing to their better natures. 'There'll be loot at the end of the fight, men,' he told them, 'and farms and estates for all of you, if we defeat Geirthjof. His lands will be our lands.'

But at the back men were beginning to run. Starkad didn't know why, but other warriors also began to hurtle through the mist. Were they under attack from the rear? Starkad followed the rest. Soon the whole war host seemed to be racing through the rocky, misty valley. Starkad, for the first time in war, felt cold hands of panic close round his heart. He had sworn not to flee from fire or iron. Now he was running blind. But from what? Not fire or iron, he was sure of that. It seemed the entire army was running from Fear itself.

They were running down a steep incline. Starkad received an impression that the rocky walls had opened up. Still the mist hung thick. Then it was gone in a twinkling.

Sun beamed down on a lush mountain valley, forests and fields on every hand. The war host of Vikar was running down the hillside towards another army, an army that was marching away from them. Starkad's fears turned to joy, and he shouted the war cry, 'Agder! Agder!'

Other men took it up, and they charged down towards the enemy.

As he ran, Starkad noticed a tall figure standing on a rocky crag, an outlier of the higher mountains. It leaned on a spear and watched their progress in approval. As they passed, it lifted the spear high and shouted in reply to the yelling warriors, 'Agder! Agder!'

It was Grani Horsehair.

3: The Battle Of The Uplands

T HE UPLANDERS PUT up a spirited defence but they had been plunged into confusion by this attack from their rear; soon they were fleeing in several directions. Bodies littered the trackway. Vikar called a halt as the remnants of the enemy force vanished into the hills.

'We'll not allow them to lure us into a bad position,' he told his men. 'We will instead begin to plunder their outlying farms and settlements, force them to meet us in the field.'

Starkad found Grani Horsehair standing beside him as he despoiled the body of an Uplander he had slain.

'Where did you go to, foster father?' he asked. 'Men thought you had betrayed us.' I thought you had betrayed us, he thought, but he didn't say it.

Grani looked at him imperturbably. 'I went ahead,' he replied. 'There was much I needed to do.'

Starkad remembered the fog that had covered the advancing army until it found itself in striking position for the now routed Upland force. He looked curiously at the old man.

'Where is it that you go, foster father?'

Grani gestured upwards. Starkad glanced up in

puzzlement. Did he mean the mountains? A raven circled the field of the fallen. That was all that he could see above them, except sky. He was about to ask the old man what he meant when Vikar joined them.

'It's not certain if King Geirthjof was with the army,' he said. 'We took prisoners but they were unhelpful. But the king's main powerbase lies in Thotn, further up in the fells, across Hringariki and Hadaland to the north east. That's where he will be heading, if he was involved in that defeat.'

'Now that the main army is scattered,' said Grani Horsehair, 'you will suffer from night attacks and hit-and-run raids. Until the Upland force regroups, you will have a hard fight of it to settle this land.'

'We have halted their attack on my kingdom, Grani,' said Vikar. 'That's the most important.' He gazed around at the great mountains and forests. 'This must be a hard place to rule,' he said, 'and it will be a harder place to conquer. But we must conquer it, or it will forever remain a threat. One day, a king will rule all these kingdoms, a high king such as rules the Swedes from Uppsala. Not just the south, either. He will rule Halogaland and the northern realms, and take tribute of furs and hides from the Lapps...'

'You truly mean to go north?' Starkad said. The men who had slain his mother and father when he was but a baby had come from Stad in Halogaland.

Vikar patted him on the shoulder. 'One day,

Starkad,' he promised. 'One day. When the south is subjugated, we will turn our eyes to the north. I do not know if it is I who will be king over the whole North Way, but if it is not me, I shall nevertheless die trying.'

'You will win many victories,' said Grani Horse-hair, 'but for every valiant man there comes a time when he is claimed by the Valkyries and taken up to Odin's hall.'

As he spoke, shouts of warning came from the scouts Vikar had posted on the edges of the war host.

Raiders had come down from the forests nearby and made an attack on the baggage train. Starkad led a group of warriors to chase them off, but they succeeded escaping with several saddlebags full of provisions.

Vikar gave orders for his forces to begin the march for Thotn. As they penetrated deeper into the mountains, small bands from the scattered Upland army made lightning raids on the war host. Night times were the worst, and Starkad got little sleep, as attack on attack was made under the cover of darkness.

Vikar's forces were being whittled down by these encounters, and the Uplanders, who were too cowardly or disorganised it seemed to face them on the open field, were sustaining fewer losses. On through the dales and thick forests they marched. They made slow progress, having to fight off almost constant attack, and it was a weary and dispirited force that came out of the forests onto the shores of the Einavatnet lake more than a week later.

They found an army awaiting them. Banners fluttered above the middle, showing the two thistle emblem of the Upland kingdom. Beside the banner bearer was a man, tall, broad-shouldered and bearded, wearing a golden circlet.

'We have found King Geirthjof,' said Vikar.

His head was bandaged from a scalp wound he had sustained in a recent fight, and his shield was battered, his cloak in tatters. Starkad and the other champions were not much better, having the lean and hungry look of so many starving wolves. The army that faced them across the flower dappled lake meadow was fresh and well-armed.

A herald stepped out from the Upland ranks.

'King Geirthjof asks what band of robbers has invaded his kingdom.'

Starkad stepped forward without conferring with Vikar.

'Tell your lord king that this band of robbers,' he called in reply, 'comes to rob him of two things. His kingdom and his life.'

'Be gone from King Geirthjof's domain,' said the herald, 'and you may take with you your lives. All but those of you who slew his brother.'

Starkad bared his teeth. 'I myself had a part in that slaying,' he said, 'but the death blow was dealt by King Vikar. He is here to contest this matter with you.'

Impatient, King Geirthjof signalled this horn blower, who blew the blast that announced an attack. The Uplanders marched forwards, beating their shields with their swords and spears.

'Attack!' Vikar cried, and the weary band of lowlanders raced across the flowers and the grassy sward to meet the foe with steel.

The battle was long and hard. Starkad strode through the ranks, sword flashing as he did so, one way and then the other, lopping off an arm here, a head there. Two spearmen came at him from either side. He leaped to evade their attacks, spun in the air and swung his sword in a glittering wheel of steel. Both men fell back, dropping their spears, clutching at new grins that gushed blood, sprayed the air with clouds of crimson mist.

At last he faced King Geirthjof.

'Why, it's the braggart who spoke for his upstart king,' roared the Uplander. 'Prepare to die, filth!'

'My name is Starkad Storverksson,' said the warrior, coming to meet the king's attack.

'I have heard of you,' said Geirthjof, as their swords met with an unmusical clang and the impact shivered up the blade into Starkad's arm. 'One of the Agder folk my brother kept as hostages for the people's good behaviour. I told him it was rash. When we three brothers set about expanding our father's domains in Hringariki, I chose to slay anyone in the countries I seized who might rival me.'

Starkad wounded him in the arm. 'Even bairns?'

Geirthjof swung a blow at Starkad's head. 'Bairns most of all,' he said as Starkad parried the attack. 'They grow up into monsters. Like you, you troll!'

Starkad swung his sword at the king's legs but he leapt lithely up and over the attack, then dealt Starkad a cut upon the cheek that bled copiously. Starkad hacked at the king who dodged and the sword sliced through his swirling cloak. Even as Starkad was hauling it out of the tangling folds, Geirthjof thrust him through the left shoulder. Starkad dropped his battered shield, then brought his freed sword up under Geirthjof's own shield, plunging into the older man's big belly.

The sword protruded from Geirthjof's back a foot. Starkad let go of the hilt and the king toppled back to land on his side in a pool of his own sticky crimson blood.

'Another king-slaying,' Starkad commented.

The Uplanders surrendered as soon as they had realised their king was dead, and Geirthjof's queen came from the nearby settlement to offer the surrender of her people. The widow queen was Ingibjorg, a young woman of no more than a score of summers, half the age of the old tyrant who had taken her as his wife after slaying her father.

'He was much hated by his people,' she confessed, speaking of her late husband with little favour as she sat on a camp chair in Vikar's pavilion. 'I was not born when he and his brothers

came out of Hringariki with their forces, but my
father told me of it when he still lived. How they
attacked the surrounding kingdoms one by one
until all the Uplands paid them tribute. The eldest
brother, Fridthjof, went on to lay Telemark under
him, giving him access to the sea, while Geirthjof
remained here in the mountains. Then the youngest went on to attack the western lands...'

Vikar pressed her small elegant hand as she
wept. 'My own father and mother were killed in
that onslaught, and I grew up an exile. We are not
so different, you and I.'

She gazed at him with melting eyes. 'What will
you do, now you have killed our king?'

He looked at her seriously. 'Now the Upland
kingdom is mine by conquest,' he said, 'but I shall
not treat you tyrannously as your husband did.'
He gave her a sidelong look.

Starkad, who had been watching the seduc-
tion uncomfortably from his king's side, broke in.
'Now that Geirthjof is dead and Fridthjof out of
the country, sire, with the full strength of his warriors, it would be a good time to seize Telemark as
well, and hold it against him on his return. He will
not be able to fight against such a large empire.'

Vikar smiled. 'You give me wise counsel as ever,
old friend. I shall leave that in your hands, foster brother, and set trusted men over these lands.
Queen Ingibjorg and I shall return to Agder, where
I hope she will honour me by accepting me as her
new husband.'

Starkad did not smile. 'Very good, sire,' he said at last.

Vikar turned to his new queen-to-be. 'This is Starkad,' he told her. 'My foster brother and foremost of my champions. He it was, giving credit where it's due, who slew your brutish husband.'

She made a face. 'I'm glad he's dead,' she confessed. 'Does that sound equally brutal?' Then she favoured Starkad with a smile that lit the tent like the dawn illumines the world. Starkad turned away and refused to look at her.

Nervously, she looked at Vikar. Pained, the king gave her an apologetic look.

'If I'm to conquer Telemark in your name,' Starkad said, 'I must start at once. I ask that you allow me to choose the best of your men. Ulf and Erp, Grettir and Sorkvir...'

Vikar gave him a sign of assent. 'Take whoever you deem fit to the wars,' he told him. 'For the moment, I intend to taste the delights of peace.' He gave Ingibjorg a broad smile, which she returned shyly. 'Oh, but Starkad,' the king added, 'we will put off the wedding until your victorious return.' Ingibjorg gave Vikar a sharp look. 'I can hardly be wed without the presence of my chief comrade in arms,' he explained.

'As you wish, sire.' Starkad strode out. As he let the tent flap fall with a thump behind him, he thought he heard the girl repeat his words in a gently mocking tone, and Vikar's laughter joined her giggles. He stalked off to choose his warriors for the coming fight.

That midsummer he was back in Agder, at the hall of his king. It was daytime, and the light of the sun filtered in through the smoke hole and glanced through the open doors. The banners hanging from the rafters were bright in its beam, and flowers had been scattered among the tapestries and blue byrnies on the walls. Delicate scents hung in the air. Men and women in festal garb stood talking in the midst of the floor, while Vikar and his queen mingled with the guests, talking and laughing.

Starkad halted in the entrance, casting a dark shadow across the bright, happy scene. Men he had fought alongside drank wine of the warm Southlands from vessels of glass, their colourful tunics hung with silks and jewellery, their women at their sides, chattering and gossiping and laughing.

Mustering his deepest resolve, gathering his dark blue cloak about himself as if to ward off the good cheer like a chill, he marched across the airy, well-lit space and halted before his liege lord, bending his head in token of fealty. The tidings he brought were ill suited to the occasion.

'My lord,' he said formally, in greetings. 'I came to your wedding as you bade me, leaving my duties in Telemark and Upland, though I was delayed. Would that I had stayed there.'

Vikar's smiling face fell at Starkad's words. Queen Ingibjorg's expression as she looked Starkad up and down was frosty. 'What do you mean by that, old friend?' He glanced from his foster brother, dressed as for war, to the laughing guests. 'Starkad,' he added, his face clearing, 'there's a time for war and a time for pleasure. And this is a time for pleasure!' He clapped his hands. 'Bring my old friend a drink.'

'Sire,' said Starkad, flexing his gauntleted hands and dismissing the approaching servant with a scowl, 'as your loyal hearth-man, I must naysay you. There is indeed a time for war and a time for pleasure, but this is not the latter. Kiss your bride, wed her and bed her and father strong sons, then saddle your horse, ready your ships and muster your levies.'

The guests had fallen silent and all looked at Starkad in trepidation.

'What means this, foster brother?' Vikar demanded.

'As I rode out of the Uplands and down the Agder road,' Starkad told the growing crowd of listeners, 'a messenger caught up with me. Listening to his words, I saw smoke, black smoke, on the horizon from the direction from which I had ridden. The messenger told me a tale of war.

'As soon as I had left, the enemy struck. Like lightning the last of the Grandsons of Fridthjof, his namesake came up from the sea, seizing Telemark and then marching into the dales of the Uplands. Men I had placed in positions of command, your own champions, have been slain. Sorkvir is reported dead, Grettir has fled before the advance. Gunnolf Blaze's fate is unknown. Two thirds of your empire are now in the hands of the enemy. I only came here to report this to you and beg of you a boon, sire, that I may lead the army of reconquest.'

The hall was silent. Vikar turned to his queen and she gazed back in silence.

4: No Quarter

S WIFT ON THE heels of Starkad's news, shortly after Vikar's hasty wedding and while the levies were still flooding in from the lands that remained under the king, came confirmation of Fridthjof's intention.

It was into a gloomy, torchlit hall that the envoy strode. Vikar sat on his high seat, Grani Horsehair, Starkad and other warriors and important men gathered before him. The space where his queen would sit was empty—feeling indisposed, she had gone to her bower while the men spoke of war. Vikar sat forwards as the envoy was led into his presence.

'Sire,' said a guard, 'here is an envoy from the sea king Fridthjof.'

'Fridthjof, king of Telemark,' the envoy corrected him. 'And now king of his brother's realm of the Uplands.' A satchel hung at the man's hip.

'What is your message?' Vikar demanded. 'Those lands are mine by right of conquest.'

'That same right has returned them into the hands you snatched them from,' the envoy said. He fumbled in the satchel, and a murmur of disquiet came from the gathered men when he flung a severed head down at the king's feet. Bloody was the stump of a neck, and bloody was the long beard. The eyes rolled back in the sockets, but Starkad from the streak of white in its fair hair knew it as the head of Gunnolf Blaze.

'My lord king's words are thus,' the envoy said, as the moans of disquiet died away. 'You hold lands that belong to him by blood right. Pay tribute and tax for these lands of which the king is lord, or suffer invasion.'

Vikar looked at him from beneath hooded lids. He called for his men.

'Take this envoy to a chamber where he can rest,' he ordered. 'Feed him and feed his horse too. Treat both well. I would not have it said that envoys do not receive a good welcome in Vikar's hall or Vikar's lands, whatever the nature of their news. In the meantime, I and my counsellors will discuss this royal message and ready our reply.'

He gestured at the severed head of Gunnolf Blaze. 'Ensure that this receives honourable burial,' he commanded.

The guards led the man outside, while servants carried away the grisly relic. Vikar asked other men to bring him his other counsellors, and told them all to meet him in the council chamber off the main hall. He hurried away to his wife's bower. She must not have the truth kept from her. Besides, he had been brought up to believe that counsel lay in women as well as men.

'My lord king,' said Queen Ingibjorg formally, standing with her handmaids as he entered. Vikar gestured to them to be at their ease and came to sit beside his wife.

'We have received messages from Fridthjof,' he told her. 'It is all as Starkad said. He tells us that we must pay him tribute if we wish for peace.'

'He is willing to give us peace?' the queen asked, clasping her hands oddly over her belly, almost as if she was protecting something. 'What will you say?'

'I will debate that with my men,' he said. 'But I thought I would also seek women's counsel.'

The queen laid slim fingers on his brawny arm, leaving her other hand clasping her belly. 'I would counsel peace,' she said. 'I would not wish our child to grow up in a time of war.'

Vikar opened his mouth to speak, but then shut it. He examined her belly to see it was indeed swelling. He had been so busy with thoughts of his kingdom his wife's condition had slipped his eye.

'A son,' Vikar said.

'Or a daughter,' she replied with a shrug.

Vikar nodded impatiently. 'If he's a boy,' he said, 'I would like to name him after my father, Harald the Agder king. And may he grow up to rule not only Agder but all the kingdoms of the North Way!'

'Harald is a good name,' the queen agreed, 'but can you not be content with what you have? See what conflict you have been dragged into by attempting to extend your realms.'

Vikar could not understand her point of view.

In combat a man can win a name that will never die. A name that will be remembered, and fastened to others in future, bringing them luck and glory. The name would live on. Perhaps it also meant the man would, too. Otherwise, of course, there was Valhalla, Odin's hall in the heavens where went warriors who died in battle.

'You counsel peace?' he asked. 'And payment of tribute?'

She nodded urgently. 'Let Fridthjof keep the fells and fjords he holds,' she said. 'Though it is the land of my forefathers, it is a hard country. Agder and your other domains are worth paying for.'

'Paying for with red gold?' he asked. 'Or with blue steel?'

She sighed. 'I would counsel gold,' she told him. 'Otherwise Fridthjof will invade, war will plague the lands, crops will be burnt, folk will starve. You would not want your son to grow up to rule a wasteland.'

Vikar left his wife's bower and went to the council chamber deep in thought.

Here waited Ulf, Grani Horsehair, Starkad, and several others, men from the kingdoms he ruled: Hordaland, Jaederen, Hardanger, and Agder itself. They greeted him as he took his place at the head of the table.

'My lords,' he said, 'we are faced with a stark choice: bow the knee and pay tribute, or fight a war with a man who rules all the Uplands and also Telemark, so he can attack by land and by sea.'

Starkad gave a disgusted noise. 'A choice?' he said. 'He offers no choice. His words are a summons to war: that is all.'

'Fridthjof has no interest in peace,' Grani Horsehair agreed. 'He is obliged to kill the killers of his brothers. The offer of peace is meant as an insult, to provoke a warm response.' He looked disapproving. 'Besides, you, sire, and your kind are in a feud with the Grandsons of Fridthjof.'

'We have fought long and hard,' Ulf said, 'to extend the bounds of our liege's lands. But perhaps we went to hastily. Overstretched ourselves.' He looked at Vikar. 'Every king of the North Way wants to become overall ruler, it seems; as the kings of Uppsala are chief kings in the lands of the Swedes. But the petty kingdoms of the North Way are separated by fjords and impassable mountains. Can one man rule over all that? Or would it be better to settle for peace with one's neighbours and to remain content with the empire you already rule?'

Vikar propped his chin in his hand. 'We have known little rest since the battle for the Uplands ended,' he said. 'Our levies have their farms to think of. They will not want to still be at the wars when it is harvest.'

Starkad shook his head. 'What does it matter what churls think, sire?' he said. 'If the food runs out we will go hunting or raiding.'

Grani Horsehair nodded. 'I will leave my farm in the hands of my thralls,' he said. 'They can bring in the harvest without me. And it will be a better harvest for knowing that the realm will not be ransacked in the name of tribute for Fridthjof.' He smacked his fist into his palm. 'Strike now, as soon as the levies can be mustered. Fridthjof is not secure in his position in the Uplands, and he has been fighting more recently than we have.'

'But he rules twice as many lands that King Vikar has,' Ulf pointed out. 'He will outnumber us. His levies will outnumber ours, and his warriors are all battle-hardened Vikings who have spent years away at sea.'

Grani Horsehair looked thoughtful. 'We must even the odds somehow,' he admitted. 'But how?'

Vikar looked up. 'I have it,' he said. 'I will send messengers to Olaf, king of the Njars. He is our ally. And his country lies on the other side of the Uplands. If he comes to our aid, attacks Fridthjof from the other flank, we can crush our enemy between us like a nut between hammer and anvil!' In his excitement, all thought of the peace his wife desired had left him.

Ulf nodded slowly, as did the other counsellors. 'That will tip the scales in our favour, sire,' he admitted. 'Shall we take a vote?'

Vikar inclined his head. 'Cast your vote, my lords,' he urged.

It was cast unanimously for war with Fridthjof. Vikar returned to the hall and summoned the envoy.

'Take this message back to your lord,' he said,

his voice echoing in the great space. 'Upland and Telemark are ours by right of conquest, and we shall meet him in the field to contest our claim. Never will my people pay tribute to him or his kindred. Now be gone from my halls and my lands!'

The messenger gave an elaborate bow, then strode from the hall. Now Vikar sent for messengers of his own and bade them take ship for Sweden and bring his word to the king of the Njars. Finally, he went to break the news to his queen.

The levies were mustered from all the lands of Vikar's fjord bitten, mountain-spined realm, gathering on the meadows outside his main settlement before sailing up the coast towards the shores of Telemark. Here they came ashore to find that the war host of Fridthjof was already awaiting them.

The Telemarkers and Uplanders appeared even as Vikar's host disembarked on the firth strand. Lines were hurriedly drawn up, but Fridthjof's force was much larger than that of Vikar, filled with troop after troop of hardy mountain men, clad in furs and byrnies and gripping big, two handed axes. The banners that flew above them bore an image of a black axe on a yellow background.

At the centre, King Fridthjof stood amidst a guard of berserks, those frenzied madmen of the Northlands who entered battle in ecstatic rages, often flinging away their armour and even their clothes as they did. Their savagery was notorious throughout the Northlands. Starkad suspected it was their malign influence that inspired Fridthjof to behead Gunnolf Blaze and send his head with that taunting message.

'What of our reinforcements?' he said to Vikar.

The king looked back at him. 'The messengers returned to say that King Olaf would join us on the field. This was the day given.'

'He is not here,' said Starkad through gritted teeth.

'My queen did not want my child to be born into a land at war,' Vikar told him.

Starkad darted a look at him. He had not known that Ingibjorg was with child. 'If you want peace, sire, you must fight for it!'

'Fight,' Vikar said, 'and die, perhaps. What then?'

Starkad shook his head. 'I do not know. I think maybe some folk are reborn. I bear my grand-father's name, he who lived in the days before Odin and his sons came down to Midgard. Some-times I dream that I am him. But we have no time for dreaming today, sire.'

Vikar turned to a herald. 'Go out and ask to par-ley,' he said. Starkad looked on incredulously.

'My lord king does not wish to see unnecessary war, Fridthjof of Telemark,' the man called to the other side. 'He bids you come to parley with him.'

'We have no time for peace,' Starkad told Vikar. 'Paying tribute will mark you as a coward. Instead we should fling ourselves into the fray and win our freedom with both hands.'

'We will parley,' the king of Telemark called out in reply. Starkad gave a disapproving grunt.

With a white shield held on a pole over them to show their peaceful intention and only a few companions, they crossed the grass to meet Fridthjof, with a similar shield held over him by one of the berserks who went with him. The king was a sinewy man of maybe two score and a half summers, who had a forked beard and eagle eyes that shot darting glances from beneath a broad brow.

'You come with this handful of fighters,' he growled, 'to beg me for peace? You could have done that from the comfort of your hall. Do you think this paltry rabble gives you a position of strength? My men could drive you back into the sea in seconds.'

'Look at that one,' sneered a black haired, bare chested, bear cloaked berserk, pointing a hairy finger at Starkad's byrnie. 'Do you think to live forever, tall man who wears ironmongery?'

'Long enough for my blade to drink its fill in your womanish breast!' Starkad roared. Vikar put a hand on his arm.

'Let us be civil,' he said. 'We want to negotiate; not begin a war we cannot hope to win here and now.'

Starkad looked at him in horrified wonder. What had happened to his old friend, the Viking, the warrior, the would-be king of the North Way?

The size of Fridthjof's host had unmanned him. He was willing to accept terms, to trade words and concessions, and not fight, for all his words of Valhalla. Was fatherhood all it took to render him spineless?

Fridthjof laughed a booming laugh, hugging at his vast chest. 'Very well, by Loki!' he cried. 'Let us negotiate. Let us decide how exactly you will give in, how you will show me your yellow belly, your white liver. I hear you took my brother's wife as your own. I liked her looks, though she never waggled her rear in my direction. Give her to me as a whore and I'll grant you concessions.'

'Very well,' said Vikar contritely. 'Aught rather than risk my men in the fray.'

'The mother of your unborn son?' Starkad couldn't believe his ears.

'Silence, man,' said Vikar curtly. Starkad retired a short space, hurt. His foster brother lacked the backbone to stand up to King Fridthjof, but he would speak to his own friend so disrespectfully?

'Go on,' Vikar told the king, who was sharing uproarious laughter with his berserks. 'What are your other terms?'

Fridthjof slapped his mailed thigh in wonder. 'My levies came here for plunder!' he barked. 'They won't like peace unless they stand to gain. What payment will you yield to each of them to make it worth their while?'

'A third of the harvest of each farm in my realm,' Vikar said. 'I do not wish to trouble your farmers.'

'A third?' Fridthjof's face purpled. 'Make that two thirds, king of the nithings!'

'Make it three thirds,' said one berserk. 'We'll beggar your kingdom and bring down a famine.'

'Make it four thirds!' bellowed another berserk, chortling, and he earned himself a scowl from his fellows.

'These terms are harsh,' Vikar observed, looking troubled. 'My subjects will be angry...'

'Accept these terms or face us in the field, poltroon!' Fridthjof said scornfully.

But even as he spoke, Starkad heard the blare of distant horns. The berserks looked about them in bewilderment.

Emboldened, Vikar drew his sword. 'I refuse your terms!' he said decisively. 'With my Njar allies, I shall fight!'

Starkad turned to see a mailed host wading up from the firth shore. Above them fluttered the crossed arrows banner of King Olaf's folk.

5: Berserk

ADOPTING A WEDGE formation, the Njar forces attacked the Uplanders on one flank. Fridthjof and his berserks retreated into the main host for the king to direct the resistance. Vikar urged on his own forces to pursue. An arrow storm darkened the sky. Arrowheads rattled on armour like hail, but it was a deadly hail and men fell beneath it.

Now the Uplanders were beleaguered. On one side, they were under assault from the Njars, on another Vikar's men attacked them—behind them a narrow, wooded valley led back into the hills, a difficult path for a sudden retreat. But now Vikar had received his reinforcements, the Uplanders and Telemarkers were outnumbered.

Starkad charged into the fray, swinging his sword left and right, followed by a spray of blood as he cut men down. It came to him that Vikar's disgraceful display of abject cowardice had been a ruse. Not only had he lulled Fridthjof, encouraged him to underestimate his opponent, he had given the latecomers from the Njar kingdom enough time to join them. Now the defenders were in trouble.

But in Starkad's mind one idea was uppermost.

He would find that sneering berserk who had fled with Fridthjof into the midst of the host and kill him.

He had heard of berserks as a boy. Grani Horse-hair had spoken well of them, saying that they made good shock troops even if they could be a liability, even attacking their own side sometimes when the berserk fit was upon them. Starkad couldn't see the sense in it, entering battle like a madman, gnawing at your shield, flinging off your byrnie.

He halted, panting. Corpses surrounded him. Men were fighting on every hand but no one came near the tall warrior. He tugged at the iron links of his hauberk. It would not be to his honour were he to meet the berserk armoured when the fool went bare chested. He hauled the byrnies off, shrugging it from his mighty shoulders. Now he was as bare chested as the berserk who had sneered at him. Gripping his sword firmly in his hand, he went hunting.

At last he found the fellow, still at the left hand of the great king of the mountains. Njars and Agder-folk surrounded the household troop as they defended their ruler. Starkad forced his way through the press until he was close to the berserk, who was glaring around him, spittle frothing at his mouth, hacking about him with an axe crimson to the haft. Bodies littered the ground at his feet, both his bear skin and his bare flesh were drenched in gore. His shield was battered, and even as Starkad watched the berserk tore at it with his teeth.

An Agder man came too close, and the berserk sprang on him with a wolfish snarl. He knocked him to the ground, held him there as he bit the man's windpipe out with his bare teeth. The berserk shuffled to his feet, glaring round him, blood all over his beard, staring blindly around him, the twitching body at his feet. Revolted, Starkad charged at him.

He swung his sword at the man's bare shoulder, and was staggered when the berserk only stood there glaring. The sword had bounced straight off his flesh!

In horror, Starkad glanced at his blade. What was wrong with it? Before he could test its sharpness, the berserk leapt at him, axe in one hand, shield in the other, teeth bared in a wolfish grin. Starkad dropped his useless sword and seized the berserk. He lifted him high then flung him at the ground. The crack of the berserk's breaking backbone was sharp enough to be audible even over the noise of the desperate fight on every hand.

He rose, picked up his sword and tested its edge. Somehow the berserk whose twisted corpse lay at his feet had blunted the blade. He brandished the useless blade as warriors passed by. Then he realised that they were fleeing the field!

To his relief, the deserters were Fridthjof's men. Many already lay on the ground, in pools of blood, dead or dying. Several of the other berserks headed for the hills. At last Fridthjof's horn blower blew a couple of dismal blasts. The Telemark standard went down and in its place was lifted the white shield of peace.

Starkad joined Vikar and his other champions for the parley—the surrender, it turned out. With them was Olaf of the Njars and his retinue. Grani Horsehair also appeared. Starkad had not seen him during the fight.

Fridthjof stalked into Vikar's presence and flung down his sword, spear and shield on the turf. With him was only a small number of his men—a paltry few, Starkad thought sardonically.

'My faithless men have fled,' Fridthjof said. 'For the most part. A few loyalists stay. Most ran when they saw your tall champion here'—he gestured languidly at Starkad— 'slay Bjorn. Never before was that berserk defeated. With a spell, he blunted the blades of his attackers. Now he lies, backbone cracked and eyes gazing sightlessly at an empty sky. Now is the backbone of my army gone, and the rest are spineless weaklings.'

'You will surrender?' asked Vikar.

'I seek an agreement between us,' said Fridthjof. 'Though we remain at feud, I will respect your rule of the fjords, of Agder and Hordaland and the other petty kingdoms. In return, you accept my rule over Telemark and the Uplands.'

'You seek terms?' Vikar said. 'You're in a poor position to do so.' Naught in his tone suggested mockery, but Starkad could not help but ponder how the two kings' situations had been reversed.

'I refuse to accept aught else,' said Fridthjof arrogantly. 'I am permitting you to keep the kingdom you took from my brother, my brother who you slew!'

'You had two brothers,' Vikar replied. 'From both of them I took kingdoms. I took your own, too, since you had abandoned it. Now, when you return to defend your possessions, I have defeated you as I did your brothers.'

Fridthjof snarled and tried to seized Vikar's throat in his hands, but his two closest hearthmen held him back. Vikar met this unflinching.

'My terms are thus,' he said. 'You yield up your kingdom, which you have lost. You acknowledge before all the folk that you renounce your possessions, you abdicate, that your lands are all mine by right of conquest. And you leave as a solitary exile.'

Starkad shivered despite himself. Wretched is the life of the exile. It seemed that the hearthmen who had held Fridthjof back agreed; they now glowered truculently at Vikar.

Fridthjof sneered and shook his head. 'Unacceptable,' he said. 'I cannot go into exile on my own. I shall take my fleet with me.'

'And then harry my coasts and my islands?' Vikar demanded. 'I will never agree to that.'

Now Olaf of the Njars stepped forward. 'I am a neutral here, for all that I weighed in on King Vikar's side,' he said. 'My kingdom lies in another land, and with the greatest respect your disagreements mean little to me—I wish only to see justice done. Will you accept my arbitration? My lord king?' he appealed to Vikar. 'Sire?' He turned to Fridthjof.

Fridthjof scorned the offer. 'I can hardly expect a fair judgement from a man who helped defeat me.'

'Peace must be made,' Vikar said, 'by the sword's edge or by men's tongues.' He glanced round at the field of slaughter. 'Enough killing has been done today. Let us see what can be achieved by talk. Let King Olaf settle this matter.'

Fridthjof shook his head. 'I refuse.'

Vikar laughed, 'You are alone, defenceless, surrounded by your foes. Even if your men rallied and returned to your side, they would still be outnumbered.'

'I vow on the oath ring of Thor that I will seek to gain you the best resolution,' Olaf said, placing his hand on the silver arm ring he wore. Starkad guessed he had taken it from the temple of that god in his own land. He shivered. He had never liked the thunder god.

Fridthjof looked grudgingly from one to the other. 'My kin have never been ones to seek wergild or settlements,' he said. 'But now I see I have no other choice.' He looked straight at Olaf. 'You will aid me?'

The Njar ruler nodded and they began their negotiations afresh under his auspices.

'Your king is a fool,' said Grani Horsehair in an aside to his foster son.

Starkad looked at him in surprise. 'Vikar a fool? What do you mean?'

'He will win naught worth the winning by this settlement,' Grani Horsehair replied. 'Rather he should fight to the finish, crush Telemark and the Uplands beneath his heel.'

'His wife is with child,' Starkad said. 'She is of the Upland race. Perhaps he seeks to spare her kin.'

Grani Horsehair turned away in disgust.

Starkad looked to see Fridthjof nodding solemnly. 'Very well,' he was saying. 'I accept these terms.'

'You will yield both kingdoms?' Vikar said.

Fridthjof looked at Olaf. 'On the condition that I am given ships and men of my choosing to join me in exile. And yes, I swear that I shall never raid the shores of your kingdom. Rather I shall take my ships westward over sea to the lands there, beyond the Northlands. Folk say the pickings are rich in those lands, and the kings are fools who squabble amongst themselves for power.' He smiled grimly. 'It will be just like home.'

Olaf nodded. 'Now shake on it,' he said, 'before all the folk.'

Vikar spat on his hand; Fridthjof did the same, and they shook like farmers or traders making a deal. Then Fridthjof turned and walked away followed by his men.

◆ ◆ ◆

Even as he was sailing away with ships and men upon the wretched path of exile, a ship with the emblem of Agder on its banner appeared in the firth. It anchored beside Vikar's ship. Men disembarked and brought him a message.

'Sire,' said their leader, 'a day ago, your wife the queen was brought to bed with the birth pangs beginning. She has given birth to two twins, boys both. The one who was eldest by a short space will be named Harald, of course. But what of your other son?'

'Two sons!' Vikar said. He clapped Starkad on the back. 'Did you hear, foster brother? I have two sons!' He turned to the messenger. 'The younger I will name Neri. Gather together all the folk. I wish to make a proclamation.'

He was raised up on a shield by his champions, Starkad included, and he called out proudly to the crowd of warriors and farmers who gathered.

'I am the father of two boys. When they reach twelve years old, my eldest, Harald, shall become king of Telemark! Until he is of age, I put the rule of the country in the hands of my champion Ulf.' The warrior named grinned up at him in wonder. 'And the Uplands shall be my younger son Neri's earldom. Until he is twelve, Erp will be its steward.'

Amid cheering, Vikar leapt down and went to

make the preparations for a victory feast.

After the feast, Olaf of the Njars parted from Vikar on the best of terms and sailed back to his kingdom. Leaving Ulf and Erp in control of the mountain realms, Vikar went back to Agder with Starkad, Grani Horsehair, and the rest of his men. Here more celebrations were prepared. During the banquet Vikar poured water over the heads of his two baby sons as Ingibjorg held them up, and he named them as he had said he would.

Starkad sat beside him on the high seat, in a place of honour. 'And my foster brother,' Vikar proclaimed to the assembly, 'who has been with me since my first oar stroke on the voyage to power, I shall make my chief counsellor and my land warden, just as his father was land warden to my own father Harald the Agder king.'

He clapped Starkad on the back and shook his hand. 'As a token of the high esteem in which I hold Starkad, I give him this ring before all the folk.' He produced a red gold arm ring that must have weighed three ounces, and slipped it onto Starkad's arm.

Starkad bowed his head, bewildered by the shouts and cries of acclaim. He rose to thank the king, but didn't know what to say. A gift needed a gift. Starkad wracked his brain for something of equal value he could give his king. He had little property other than that which his king had given him. But he was not wholly a pauper.

'In return, I give to my king before all the folk,

Thruma Island which his father gave my father—for his and his progeny to hold in perpetuity!'

He sat down again, sweating and feeling he had made a poor showing, and the banquet went on in a haze of ale and mead and wine and bread and pork and beef.

He was uncomfortable in these surroundings. Since Vikar came to him where he lazed beside the fire in Grani Horsehair's house, all he had known was desperate fighting, glorious victories and miserable defeats, once after another, kingdoms gained and lost and gained again, wars and battles on sea and land. Now it was all over, it seemed, and he had regained all that he had lost so long ago that he had no recollection of it.

He had been no older than Vikar's sons when the Vikings from Halogaland—his own uncles—had come to avenge the abduction of their sister by killing both her and her abductor, Starkad's father. Somehow, he had survived the destruction of the farm on Thruma Island and been taken in by Harald the Agder king. His earliest memories were of being fostered alongside Vikar, but that had not lasted when Agder was conquered by Herthjof...

When he had learned of his father and mother and their death at the hands of the Halogaland Vikings, he had told himself that when he had the chance, he would gain revenge. He remembered that he had spoken of this with Vikar, shortly after the king had seized power over Hordaland—the first oar stroke on his voyage to power.

As Vikar sat down beside him, having drained an aurochs' horn of mead in a single gulp, Starkad looked at him seriously.

'Sire,' he murmured. 'A boon.'

'Foster brother,' Vikar said, looking glassily at him, and giving a drunken laugh, slapping Starkad on the arm. 'Ask aught of me.'

'Long ago,' Starkad said, 'when you were king of Hordaland only, I spoke to you of a matter of revenge. The killers of my kin remain at large, to my knowledge. I would hunt them down and avenge the death of my father and mother. I would bring them the death of the blood eagle. You said you would sail north once you had taken on the east. Now that the east is at your feet, I ask that we sail north.'

Vikar looked at him, suddenly sober. 'Old friend,' he said, 'we will indeed sail north. We will seek out your father's killers, if they still live, and wreak vengeance on them. I swear it. But not yet. There's a kingdom to rule, an empire, and I need you at my side while I firm myself upon my throne. Once that is done, once my sons are old enough to take their own places in the kingdom, I will sail north with you on the trail of vengeance.'

He rose. 'Bring the oath ring from the temple of Thor,' he called, and it was done with haste. 'before all the folk and in the name of all the gods, of Thor and Odin and Frey,' the king swore, 'when my rule is fully established in these lands and my sons are of age, I will take my ships north to Halogaland in search of the killers of Starkad's father.' He clapped Starkad on the back. 'And together we will gain vengeance—and victory!'

Everyone cheered. Everyone but Starkad, who gazed up at the king in silence.

6: Casting The Runes

TWELVE YEARS HAD passed since Vikar's victory over the king of the Uplands.

Twelve long years. As they passed like autumn twilight, Starkad slowly grew used to his new life as land warden. Peace reigned over the kingdom, apart from occasional raids and attacks from Vikings. These gave Starkad an opportunity to keep his fighting skills well honed, but they were fewer than he would have liked.

King Vikar seldom took part in the fights, and he never led his people on raids into other territories. He seemed wholly taken up with rearing children and raising crops, ensuring the prosperity of his kingdom. He even offered sacrifices to the Vanir gods, Frey and Freya and Njord and the rest, deities Starkad privately regarded as unmanly. Starkad seldom muddied his own boots in the fields. Nor had he married, despite Vikar's urging, not wanting to sully himself with a woman, or with child rearing.

He worried about Vikar. One day they would sail north on the quest for vengeance, but would so many years of peace not unman the king? As he reached his mid-twenties, Starkad looked back on a life that had seen more peace than seemed right for a man such as he. After the adventurous empire-building years of his youth, the life of warding the king's tranquil land came as an anticlimax.

At times, he thought of taking the ships and men that were his to command as land warden and sailing north in search of the killers of his father and mother. But he knew that if he did that, he would make Vikar an oath breaker. If he avenged his father on his own, Vikar could never aid him, as he had sworn. Oath breaking, treachery —these were not the ways of a true man.

Was farming? To Starkad's mind, agriculture was best left to the race of thralls. It was for such work that the god known as Rig the Walker had fathered such folk in the morning of the world. Warriors such as his king should never lower themselves to grubbing in the soil. Hunting was the best way to provide food—it was a war of a kind, a war against the beasts, and Starkad spent much time hunting, but it wasn't the same as war. The years of peace robbed a man of his backbone. Sometimes he felt that his own spine was as limp as that of the berserk he had killed at that last great battle where Vikar's empire was forged.

Sometimes Grani Horsehair visited his foster son, sailing down from Fenhring in Hordaland. Other times he was mysteriously absent for long periods, even several years at one point. But Starkad was used to these strange absences. He remembered people had thought Grani might be a traitor. Even Starkad had doubted him in the days of war. But now he thought he knew why Grani spent so long away from the kingdom.

'Would that my duties permitted me to sail away on brave exploits,' Starkad said bitterly, one evening with the grizzled old warrior—grizzled, aye, but no more so than Starkad remembered him from his childhood. 'I must sail along the coasts and ward my liege lord's lands.'

'You do see some fighting, foster son,' Grani said. 'Last summer you were hailed as the hero of the kingdom when you routed that Viking fleet.'

Starkad sighed. 'I was not made for peace, foster father. And I have the deaths of my mother and father to avenge.'

'And what then?' Grani asked. 'If ever you achieve your vengeance, where will you sail?'

Starkad could not answer. So long had his life been fixed on the point of vengeance for his mother and father that he could see no further.

It was the following year that Harald Vikarsson and his brother Neri came of age, and were old enough to take up their duties in Vikar's empire. Shortly after, Starkad received a summons from the king. Vikar intended to fulfil his oath.

'We shall sail north into Halogaland,' the king told him; 'my whole fleet, apart from those who remain to defend the realm. Ulf will stay here, as land warden in your stead. The rest of us shall sail for Halogaland.'

'And when we are there,' said Starkad, smacking a gauntleted fist into a gauntleted palm, 'we shall hunt down the killers of my kin and put them to the sword.'

Two moons later, a hundred longships set sail from the Agder coast, bright daubed sails bellying in the sea breeze, and began to make their slow way up north, hugging the shore, sailing through the channels between the uncountable islands, passing the fjords of the mainland on the right hand. They met no resistance as they went, although at times they surprised smaller groups of Viking ships that fled at their advance.

By night they would anchor off a skerry or small island, or within a remote firth, with the awnings pulled up over the decks and the cooking fires on the shore lighting the scene with a ruddy glow. Starkad had his own ship, and several other vessels in the fleet were under his command, but he sailed due abaft of Vikar's great dragon ship, Herthjof's Gift, an ironic name for a vessel Vikar had taken from the dead king of Hordaland years before, when he and Starkad were young and hungry.

'All I know of the killers of my kin is that they were sons of the earl of Halogaland,' Starkad told Vikar, 'and they came from Stad. They must be old by now.'

Even if they were greybeards, he told himself, like Grani Horsehair, he would still slay them. Besides, they were killers of their own kin, an even worse crime. They had killed their own sister for eloping with his father, Storverk.

'It may be an easy matter to find them,' said Vikar. 'Or it may be very hard. Styr and Steinthor came from Stad, but they are long gone.' Few of the men who had been with them in the early days remained. 'Few folk still live who remember the old days when we were but babes.'

Starkad shrugged. 'Grani Horsehair still lives. He seems never-changing.'

Vikar sent a man to find the lean old greybeard and soon Grani Horsehair was with them.

'I remember little,' he said. 'I was King Herthjof's warrior in those days, and Agder was beyond the margins of his realm. It was only later that he conquered it. As for Halogaland, I had kin there once. Perhaps they are still there. I have kin in many places.'

Starkad was intrigued. He had never heard Grani Horsehair mention his kindred before. This was odd, he now realised. Perhaps having kin so widely scattered explained his regular and prolonged absences.

'We are sure to meet some resistance,' Vikar said, 'but we have the strength to negotiate what we want—the yielding up of Fjori and Fyri, sons of the earl.' His eyes narrowed. 'It may mean war. But we're used to that. If the gods are with us, we shall gain our goal.'

Grani Horsehair smiled enigmatically at this

but made no comment.

The next morning, the wind had changed. It blew southwards, against them. Starkad stood at the bow, staring at the wooded island where they had anchored. It was uninhabited, although here and there ancient standing stones loomed among the bushes. He looked up into the welkin. The wind did not look likely to change. It was as if the gods had been listening, but not with any favour.

Vikar came over from his dragon ship to join him. 'The wind will change,' he said confidently. 'Until then, we have the oars.'

'You can't ask the men to row all the way against the wind to Halogaland,' Starkad told him.

Vikar gritted his teeth. 'I thought it was you who wanted to go there. I'm leading my fleet to war in Halogaland for your sake.'

'We swore vows long ago,' said Starkad. 'I fight for you, I never retreat from fire or iron. In return you look after my welfare.'

'I gave you gold and honours,' said Vikar.

'But I want vengeance.' Starkad toyed with the arm-ring Vikar had given him.

The frustration was telling on both. The sun beat down as the two old friends glowered at each other.

Grani Horsehair joined them. 'The wind is against us,' he observed.

'Thank you, I had noticed,' said Vikar bitingly. 'We can only wait for it to change.'

'There's something unnatural about this wind,'

said Starkad. 'I've sailed these sea lanes for many years and I've never known the wind to be like this. We can only raise the awnings, break out the rations, and wait until it changes.'

'Very well,' said Vikar. 'There is no way of getting to Halogaland in this wind, I see that now.' He shrugged. 'We must wait until the wind changes.'

'But what if it doesn't change?' asked Grani Horsehair.

Starkad stared at him. His foster father seemed very calm, but he sensed hidden currents beneath the surface.

'It will change,' said Vikar with the certainty of a man who had carved out an empire early in life. 'It must change, sooner or later.'

'We'll see,' said Grani Horsehair. He returned to his ship and Vikar went to his own. Starkad stood on his own deck in the buffeting wind and pondered his foster father's words.

The following day the wind was still against them, and it seemed to be growing stronger. Vikar called a council of war on the nearby island which Starkad and Grani both attended along with the chief men of the fleet.

'The wind has been against us for two days,' said Vikar, standing with his foot on the stump of a felled tree. 'We can wait for it to change, but who knows how long that will take? Otherwise we have no way of reaching Halogaland. As luck would have it, we are still within my kingdom, so we need have fear of attack. But for the moment our expedition is stymied.'

'This is a bad business,' grumbled one man. 'I don't like this wind. There's something unnatural about it.'

'It is sent by the gods,' said another man, rolling his eyes. 'Someone amongst us has angered the gods.'

Vikar shook his head. 'I have given the gods their due,' he argued. 'They cannot be angry with me.'

Starkad felt uneasy at the mention of the gods. It was true that the wind seemed unnatural, but was it sent by the gods? If so, why?

'How can we know if the gods are behind this?' he asked. 'And how can we fend off their ire, should it be them?'

'We must cast the runes,' said Vikar. 'Only that way can we hope to learn what the gods desire.'

'Cast the runes?' Starkad felt mounting horror. Never had he meddled in sorcerous matters. He did not want it said in his saga that he had relied upon uncanny means to win his ends, only that he believed in his might and main as a man should. 'Who here knows how to write the runes, or to read them, let alone cast them?'

'I know how to read the runes,' said Grani Horsehair quietly. 'I know how to write them, aye, and how to cast them too.'

Starkad looked at him in shock. He was certainly learning new things about the man who had raised him.

'Then it is you who must cast them,' said Vikar simply.

Grani Horsehair took a bough from a beech tree that grew on the island and with his knife cut it into slips of wood, each of which he marked with a different rune, reddening it with the blood of a calf that the crew of a longship had slaughtered preparatory to eating it. There were sixteen rune-marked slips in total. He gathered them up into a white cloth then cast them on the ground.

Starkad watched uneasily as his foster father lifted his gaze heavenwards, and, muttering invocations, lifted first one, then another, then a third rune-marked slip of beech. Now he inspected each one closely.

'What do they tell you?' Vikar asked impatiently.

Grani regarded him. 'The gods will end this wind only when a man from your war host is given to Odin. He must be hanged by the neck as a human sacrifice. He must be chosen by lot.'

No one spoke. Only the wind moaned and wailed, stirring up the waters out to sea into towering waves.

'Very well, then,' said Vikar. 'A man from the host, you say? We must all draw lots?' He looked about him. 'Tell the men to come ashore,' he said.

It took a long time for all the men to come ashore, and the afternoon was almost over before finally they were gathered there on the strand. Vikar stood before them and explained what had happened, and what they had learnt when Grani Horsehair cast the runes.

'I want everyone to take a lot,' he said, 'and make their mark upon it. See, here I scratch my name on this piece of wood.' He took off his golden helmet and cast it in. 'All of you do likewise.'

Starkad knew little about runes, but he knew how to write his name, so with his dagger he inscribed it upon a sliver of wood, and dropped it into the king's helmet. The men lined up and walked past Vikar, each dropping in his lot.

Now they reassembled in front of the king. With a flourish, Vikar held the golden helmet out, then, gazing skywards as Grani had done earlier, he reached in and took out the first piece of wood his fingers found.

'Read it out, sire,' Grani said. 'Whose name is inscribed there?'

Vikar looked up, stricken, his face corpse white. 'It says "Vikar",' he replied. 'It's my lot. Death by hanging. My lot.'

Starkad gave a bark of laughter. 'Nay,' he said. 'It's absurd. The gods can't expect us to sacrifice our own king! Our own war leader! Put the lot back in and choose again. No, let me choose.'

'Nay,' said Grani Horsehair. 'The gods have spoken. Vikar is chosen. He was chosen long ago. He must hang.'

Starkad stared at his foster father in disbelief.

7: The Gods In Judgement

NIGHT FELL, AND they returned to the ships. Starkad's mind was in confusion. They could hardly be expected to sacrifice the king for a good wind. It was impossible. They were in a cleft stick. They had to keep sailing; they couldn't go back home, defeated by the elements; nor could they offer up their own king and war leader in sacrifice to the gods.

Starkad ate a scanty meal of stock fish and went to lie down on his deck, surrounded by his sleeping warriors. An uneasy silence hung over the ships, broken only by the creak of timbers and the thrum of the rigging, muted conversation from sentries or from men eating together, while the howl of the contrary winds was still audible from out to sea. The night sky arched overhead, glittering with malignant stars. Starkad slept, bundled in his cloak, but his dreams were troubled.

He woke suddenly. Something dark stood between him and the starlight. Starkad sat up, panting. He felt a hand on his shoulder.

'It's me,' said a voice. It was Grani Horsehair.

Starkad rose. In the starlight, the slumbering forms of his men dotted the deck, and around them he could dimly make out the other ships riding in the roadstead. Grani Horsehair wore a long dark cloak and wore a hood over his head. From beneath it Starkad could see only the glint of a single eye.

'Come with me, Starkad,' the old man whispered.

He led Starkad to the side where a small rowing boat bobbed in the water. First Grani, then Starkad jumped down onto the deck of the little vessel, and Grani cast off.

They sailed to the shore of the island and Grani took a spear from where it lay on the deck of the boat and holding it in one hand led his foster son into the woods. There was no moon, only the dim starlight, and everything was hung with shadow. It was cold, too, and Starkad's breath steamed in the air before him.

The journey seemed to go on forever. Grani led Starkad down a narrow forest path, as the wind soughed in the trees above them, seeming to know exactly where he was going. Starkad did not know, could not guess. He wanted to stop his foster father and ask him where he was leading him, on this dark, uncertain, never ending path. But somehow the words froze in his throat, and he could not speak or demand a halt.

At last they came into a clearing. To Starkad's surprise it was packed with people, anonymous dark forms, mysterious in the starlight. In the centre of the clearing stood twelve wooden chairs, elaborately carved like the high seats of kings. Eleven were occupied. The last and biggest was empty.

Grani led Starkad through the silent throng. Leaving Starkad standing before them, he went to sit on the empty chair. The occupants of the other chairs welcomed him.

'Odin!' they called. 'Hail Odin! Hail!'

Grani—or Odin? —inclined his head in acknowledgment of their greetings. 'We must shape the weird of Starkad,' he told them.

In silence, Starkad examined the silent throng behind him, at the other men on the chairs. On one side of Grani sat a big fellow with a red beard. Propped against his chair was a large, short handled hammer. Something about this man filled Starkad with dread.

On Grani's left was a youth with a short, jutting beard who wore a pointed cap. While all the others wore swords at their hips or carried some other weapon, he had none. Beside him was an older man with a white beard. Next a young warrior who was missing his right hand. Then a man with a harp lying in his lap. Next was a curly haired fellow whose teeth glinted as if they were made of gold. Another was notable for the size of his shoes. Another had a bow, and skis were propped against his chair. Before Starkad could look at all the men who sat in judgement over him, the red bearded man spoke.

'Starkad's grandmother chose a wily giant as her husband rather than the god Thor. I shape

Starkad's weird: he shall have neither son nor daughter, and his line shall end with him.'

Grani looked sternly at the speaker.

'I shape his weird; he shall live three lifespans.'

The red bearded man threw his head back defiantly. 'He shall commit a niddering deed in each life.'

Grani replied: 'I shape his weird: he shall always have the best clothes and weapons.'

'I shape his weird,' said Red Beard, 'that he will never own land or farms.'

'I shape it that he shall never lack for money,' said Grani.

'He shall never think he has enough,' said Red Beard.

'I give him this weird, victory in every fight,' said Grani.

'I give him this,' said Red Beard, 'that in every fight he shall receive a severe wound.'

'I give him this,' said Grani, 'the art of poetry. He shall be able to compose verse as fast as he can speak.'

'I give him this,' said Red Beard, 'he shall never remember the poems he composes.'

'I shape this as his weird,' said Grani; 'he shall be loved by the nobility and kings.'

'But he shall be hated and detested by the common folk,' said Red Beard. He folded his arms and glowered at Grani.

That seemed to end the contest. Grani—or whoever Starkad's foster father truly was—looked about him. 'Now shall you pass sentence,' he directed them.

The gathered judges conferred for some time. Starkad stood in silence, awaiting their decision. Red Beard glared at him in disfavour. Again he shuddered. It was as if he had met this fellow before. Somehow, he knew that if that had been the case, they had not been friends.

At last one of the judges, who wore the sign of the balance on his tunic, rose and said, 'Our finding is that everything Thor and Odin have said shall come true. Meeting dismissed.'

Everyone rose from their chairs and began to leave. The throng broke up. Starkad stood in the middle of the clearing, alone and uncertain. Grani joined him.

'Come with me, foster son,' he said.

Starkad followed him from the clearing. As they went he looked back. Apart from the ghostly shapes of the twelve chairs standing in the starlight, there was no sign anyone had ever been there.

In silence, he walked after his foster father down the winding forest path. His mind was aflame with questions but again he found it impossible to put them into words. What had happened in the clearing? Why had judgment been made upon him? What had he done?

He remembered those dreams that had plagued him since childhood. It was then that he knew where he had seen Red Beard before. In his dreams.

In his dreams, he had fought him, but… he didn't know how the fight ended. Always he would awaken, just as Red Beard swung his hammer at him.

They had called him Thor.

The judges in the clearing had called him Thor. And they had hailed Grani Horsehair as Odin. Odin, chief of the gods, whose relationship with his red bearded son Thor was said to be a troubled one. Odin had slain the frost giant Ymir in the morning of the world. Some said he had built up the entire cosmos from the giant's dismembered corpse. The sky was Ymir's skull, the rocks and stones his teeth, the mountains his bones, the salt sea his blood. Starkad had always thought that this was little more than poetry.

But generations ago, Odin and his fellow gods had come to Midgard, the world of men, settling at Uppsala in the country of the Swedes. Odin had ruled over the northern world and made his sons kings beneath him. The rulers of Halogaland were said to descend from Saeming Odinsson, the Danes from his son Skjold. At the end of a long life in this mortal realm, by Odin returned to Asgard, heavenly world of the gods, hanging himself before all the folk and stabbing himself with his own spear— and ever since then, when men were sent to Odin as sacrifices, the same rite was repeated.

Had Odin returned from Asgard?

They came out of the trees at the edge of the strand. The moon had risen while they were in the depths of the forest, and now it poured its silver light on the ships as they rested at anchor in the bay. Still the wind, which whipped at Starkad's beard and hair, was against them.

They stood under the eaves of the forest. Grani Horsehair turned to Starkad.

'Now you can repay me, foster son,' he said, 'for the aid I have given you.'

Starkad looked inquiringly at him. He felt as if he was in a dream. Perhaps he would awaken to find himself wrapped in his furs on the deck of his ship.

'You must find some way to send King Vikar to me,' Grani said.

Starkad stared at him. 'Why must I give Vikar to you, and not some other king?'

'The grey wolf gapes,' said Grani, 'at the halls of the gods. Besides, he was promised to me long ago. His mother vowed him to me before he was born.'

The following morning, as decided, the counsellors met again to continue their deliberations. They could not sacrifice the king to the gods, even for a good wind to Halogaland. But something had to be done.

Starkad stood up before them, leaning on a thick reed.

'I have had a plan,' he told the others. 'It came to me last night, as I walked in the forest, pondering the matter.'

'I couldn't sleep either,' said Vikar. 'I saw you going ashore as I looked out from the fo'c'sle of my ship. Who was that with you?'

'It was my foster father,' Starkad replied. He looked about him.

'Strange,' said Vikar. 'There is no sign of Grani Horsehair today. Perhaps he has gone on one of his journeys.'

'Perhaps,' said Starkad. 'My plan, sire, is this.' He took them to a fir. Beside it was the stump of a felled tree. A narrow branch of the fir ran up to somewhere near its crown.

'We hang you from this fir,' he said.

The counsellors muttered darkly, and even Vikar stared at Starkad in concern.

'You will hang me?' he said.

Starkad pointed to the strand where the cooks had slaughtered another calf from the fleet's stores in preparation to cook it. 'Someone bring me the guts from that carcase. The intestines would be best.'

A guard marched over and soon returned with a downturned smile and the calf's guts dangling from his hand. Starkad stepped up onto the tree stump and took hold of the narrow branch, bending it down, then tying to it one end of the long pink rope of intestines. The other end dangled on the ground. Starkad hauled it up and tied a noose in it.

'Now your gallows is ready for you, sire,' he told Vikar, 'and I don't think it looks too risky. Come over here and let me slip this noose round your neck.'

Vikar crossed over to where Starkad stood holding the noose of guts.

'If this contraption is no riskier than it looks,' said Vikar, 'I don't think it will do me any harm. If things turn out otherwise, then the Norns must shape my weird.'

He got up onto the tree stump next to Starkad, and his old friend slipped the clammy noose over his neck, then stepped down with the aid of the reed he had in his hand, holding the fir branch down with the other.

He levelled the reed as he had seen men hold spears when sacrificing men to the king of the gods, and said the traditional words: 'Now I give you to Odin.' He thrust the reed at Vikar.

The reed sank into Vikar's flank. The king clutched at it in horror and as he did so his feet slipped and he fell from the trunk. Starkad let go of the branch and it yanked the king's struggling form up into the air where he dangled from the intestines as if it was a real rope, the reed jutting from his side like a spear.

The crowd fell silent. Silence descended on the island. Even the birdsong from the forest died away. A cloud passed over the sun and the land lay dark and cold and silent. Silent except for the creak of the tree as Vikar's lifeless body danced at the end of the gallows rope.

8: Stranded

'HE'S KILLED THE king.'

'He's killed the king! Starkad's killed the king! The traitor!'

'Starkad the traitor! Starkad's killed the king!'

'Look!' Starkad pointed to the ships. Now the wind was swelling their sails. 'The wind has changed. Odin has accepted the sacrifice! Now we can sail north!'

No one listened. 'He's killed the king…! …killed the king! Traitor!… traitor!'

The leaders of the host stood before him like hounds baiting a great black bear, their men crowding up behind them, gaping up at the slowly swinging dead weight that hung from the tree. Starkad glared down at them. He thought he could fight them all. But the realisation of what he had done unmanned him. He glanced up at the body of Vikar. His king. His foster brother. His friend.

He drew his sword and ran at these little men, brandishing it at them. Frightened, the warriors gave way. The sand was crowded with men. Even he couldn't hope to cut his way through all of them. But he had a direct path towards the edge of the woods. It didn't look like he would be sailing to Halogaland in a hurry. He sheathed his sword, veered left and vanished into the forest.

Emboldened by his flight, angry warriors from the host crashed through the bushes and undergrowth on his heels. He ran on and on, till the breath sobbed from his lungs. He continued running. He ran from the warriors. He ran from what he had done.

Now he was an exile, an outcast. Now he was cut off from his folk, from mankind. He had killed his own king, the worst crime a warrior could ever commit. It was not unknown; some kings had seized power that way, but seldom was their reign an easy one. Hearth-men who killed their king were reviled, hated, by the nobility and the commonalty alike. It was their lot to wander the roads of exile until they died a wretched death.

The sounds of pursuit were still audible when he burst from the trees on the far side of the island. In fact, they were growing louder. But Starkad stood stock still on the strand, gazing at the water before him, head cocked to listen to the shouts that floated to him from the woods.

'...this way... we've found his trail... he went this way...'

But Starkad's attention was drawn by the small boat that lay at anchor before him, and the tall, hooded man who sat on its aft thwart.

'I need your boat,' he said. He put his hand on the hilt of his sword. 'I will pay my passage with steel.' The sounds of pursuit were growing louder.

'Come aboard,' came a rusty old voice. 'I will ferry you to the mainland.'

He leapt aboard and the man began to row. Starkad looked back to see men running down onto the sand, their spears glittering in their hands. They halted at the water's edge, apart from a few who leapt in and swam after them. But the old man was a strong rower for all his age and made rapid progress. Soon the island was a dot on the horizon and the pursuing warriors were out of sight.

'You are a runaway.'

Starkad turned to look at the hooded old man. He couldn't make out his face. The voice that emanated from the cowl sounded as if it came from beneath the grave, from some ancient burial mound ribbed with the bones of the dead and crawling with grave worms. He couldn't tell if the words were a question or a statement.

'Thanks, old man,' he said courteously. 'I am a fugitive. Few men would aid me. I killed my lord.'

'Why?' asked the cowled figure. Mist now rolled across the sea, surrounding them. Starkad had no idea of where they were going. He wondered if the old man knew.

'I wanted vengeance,' Starkad said after a short pause to collect his chaotic thoughts. 'I wanted vengeance, and the wind was against us. The gods demanded a sacrifice. The king was chosen. He was my friend! My foster brother! I sacrificed him by trickery. The wind changed, but every man's hand was against me. I will still win through, though. I will hunt down the killers of my kin and slay them by the blood eagle. I have sworn this. And I will make any sacrifices to achieve my goal.'

'Vengeance of kin is a man's first duty,' the old man wheezed.

'But I swore to follow my lord in all things, to guard him in battle, never to flee from fire and iron, not to outlive him.' He looked moodily out to sea. 'And then there were the gifts I received. In return for the betrayal of my lord.'

'You were suborned?' asked the old man.

Starkad grimaced. 'You wouldn't understand. The gifts... There were curses, too...! I didn't understand it.' No one would ever believe what he had seen in that clearing deep in the forest of that wooded isle. He wouldn't speak of it.

In a silence broken only by the gentle splash of the oars, they rowed across the misty strait.

Starkad broke the still. 'Why Vikar?' he muttered to himself. 'Why Vikar, of all kings?'

'The grey wolf gapes at the hall of the gods,' the old man replied in a clear voice, with none of its earlier quavering. He shook his head back and the cowl fell away from his face. It was Grani Horsehair.

'Foster father!' Starkad exclaimed. 'What are you doing as a ferryman?' Then he remembered. 'But you're not Grani, are you? You're not my foster father.' For the first time, he noticed that Grani had only one eye. 'You're him!'

'I am Odin,' the ferryman confirmed. 'I am also your foster father.'

'You truly are Grani?' Starkad was bewildered.

'I always was Grani,' the ferryman replied. 'But in Asgard they call me Odin.'

'Is that where you were?' Starkad demanded. 'All those times when you were gone, when I was a lad? You were in Asgard?'

'And other worlds too,' said Grani. 'My journeys take me to all the worlds there are.'

'Other worlds,' Starkad said. He thought he might be crossing the waters of some other world. Land was still shrouded by the mist, if it was truly out there.

'It's this world that concerns you,' Grani said. 'The world of men. We call it Midgard.'

'Then we're still in... Midgard?' Starkad asked.

'Oh, yes,' Grani said. 'At the Thing, you have been proclaimed outlaw and wolf's head. All men's hands will be against you for the killing of the king.'

'I killed him,' Starkad said, 'my old friend, foster brother, and comrade in arms—because the wind was against us, and it was the only way it would be changed.'

'The wind has changed,' Grani said. 'And Vikar has been claimed, as was promised long ago.'

'Is that all you care about?' Starkad couldn't understand.

'You were paid for your treachery in advance,' Grani told him. 'You have my blessings. The blessings of a god.'

'I have the curses of a god, too,' said Starkad. 'Or had you forgotten? Your son Thor has cursed me. A curse for every blessing! Why?'

Grani fixed him with that single glittering eye.

'You have lived before,' he said. 'You know it, don't you? The memory has haunted your dreams since you were young.'

Starkad stared into space.

'I remember ice fields, endless ice fields,' he murmured. 'I remember fighting. I remember abductions, wars, duels.' He looked at Grani. 'I remember being killed. Thor killed me!'

'In another life, you were the troll-spawned Starkad the Giant,' Grani said dispassionately. 'You slew both trolls and men, carried off women, and at last came into conflict with my son. Over a woman.'

'Thor said something about my grandmother preferring a troll over himself,' Starkad recalled.

Grani chuckled. 'A little unfair,' he said. 'Alfhild, the elven princess, was promised to Thor, but you, in your previous life, carried her away to your cave in the world of men.'

'I lived in a cave?' Starkad was revolted. 'I truly was a troll, then.'

'Things were more rough and ready in those days,' Grani said. 'The princess was used to better, though. Her father prayed to Thor and Thor came after you. He slew you as he has slain many giants. I remember he boasted about it in Valhalla afterwards. He boasts often.'

'And so he cursed me?' Starkad said. 'For something I did in another life? But you blessed me—if those were truly blessings. Why?'

'Because you are my foster son,' Grani replied. 'And for the reason already given. You sent Vikar to me. Now he is one of my Einherjar, my warriors who feast in Valhalla. The grey wolf gapes at the halls of the gods. One day Ragnarok will come. The Doom of the Gods. We shall fight until the end. The more warriors I have in my host, the longer it will take the forces of chaos to conquer, and destroy the worlds.

'Vikar's mother once prayed to me, when she had a rival for her royal husband's affections, an older wife. They were set to brewing and the king said he would keep the wife who was the best brewer. Her rival prayed to Freya, I believe, but Vikar's mother—and this was before Vikar was born—called upon me. I promised her victory in return for that which lay between her and the brewing vat. She consented eagerly, little knowing that soon she would be big with child. That child was born and splashed with water and named Vikar.'

'You cheated her,' Starkad said. 'You cheated her like you cheated me.'

'I cheated you?' Grani echoed his words.

'You said you would take Vikar and in return the wind would change.'

'The wind did change, foster son.'

'But now I am an outcast!' he said. 'Now I can no longer sail with the fleet to Halogaland and find the killers of my kin and wreak vengeance on them! I shall have to go alone, on the wretched paths of exile, searching for them by myself.'

Grani shook his head. 'I would not counsel that,' he said.

'Why not?' Starkad asked. 'Would you make me an oath breaker?'

'Your weird will lead you elsewhere,' Grani said. 'Besides, you could never fulfil that oath.'

'Why not?' Starkad repeated.

'A few nights after they descended on your father's farm and slew him and your mother and everyone there except you, who they overlooked,' Grani said, 'your uncles' ship struck a rock and went down with all hands. They died over twenty-five years ago.'

The keel of the boat scraped against sand and a shock went through the timbers as if they too had struck a hidden rock. The mist was clearing, and Starkad saw that they had come ashore. Grani shipped his oars and gestured to him to disembark.

'What do I do now?' the outlaw asked, standing on the shore as Grani remained sitting.

'Follow this strand southwards,' Grani said. 'In a secluded inlet, you will find the ships of a Viking fleet belonging to two sea kings, Beimuni and Frakki.' He pushed off, still speaking. 'Frakki has decided to settle down, and Beimuni is looking for a new partner to voyage with. That partner will be you, Starkad.'

It was a chance. Perhaps the only chance, now that he was an outlaw. To join a Viking host wholly independent of any kingdom, the fleet of a sea king. But could Starkad trust the man—the god—now disappearing into the mist that still hung over the sea?

'Will he take me on?' Starkad said. 'I am the killer of my lord.'

'Kings and lords and nobles will always love you, Starkad.' The voice was faint as its owner vanished into mist and mystery. 'Go with my blessings, foster son.'

The mist swallowed him up. Turning, Starkad loped southward down the strand.

The story continues in
'Starkad The Outcast'.

BOOKS IN THIS SERIES

Starkad Omnibus

Starkad The Outcast

Blessed by Odin, cursed by Thor, Starkad was doomed to wander the world for three lifespans, committing a villainous act in each. Hated by the people, loved by murderers and tyrants, he sought only peace, but his destiny was endless war...

The legendary viking warrior battles his way through three more savage adventures in the lands of Norse mythology:

STARKAD THE WANDERER

Three short stories chronicling Starkad's wanderings after his banishment from the kingdom of his birth:

The Laws of the Vikings

Shapeshifter
Sons of Frey

STARKAD THE DESERTER

Now a trusted retainer of the sea king brothers Haki and Hagbard, Starkad ploughs the waves in search of glory and plunder, until Haki resolves to settle down. After leading his forces to conquer Sweden, King Haki devotes his time to ruling that decadent land in peace.

Starkad, Hagbard, and the rest turn their backs on such womanish sloth and return to the Viking way. Yet will their own adventures upon the waters of the East Way, in the fields of war and of love, doom Haki's hard won kingdom?

STARKAD THE PEACEBREAKER

Rescued from the storm by the Saxon king Frodi, Starkad becomes land warden of an empire that includes Saxon and Danish dominions. After the Danes throw off the Saxon yoke and slay Frodi, Starkad is sickened to see his son and successor neglect his filial duty as far as to make peace with the Danes. There is even talk of a marriage alliance between the two royal houses.

Unwillingly Starkad keeps the peace, until he can contain himself no longer. His vengeful actions will spell the destruction of halls and kingdoms.

Starkad The Old

Blessed by Odin, cursed by Thor, Starkad was doomed to wander the world for three lifespans, committing a villainous act in each. Hated by the people, loved by murderers and tyrants, he sought only peace, but his destiny was endless war...

The legendary viking warrior battles his way through three more savage adventures in the lands of Norse mythology:

STARKAD AT THE BRAVIC WAR

Peace lies over the Northlands. Their overlord is the ageing king, Harald Wartooth, who united the lands in his youth and has lived into old age. Starkad is just one of many warriors who bend the knee in fealty to the old king. But peace is not the way of the Viking, nor is it the way of Odin, king of the gods.

Soon war will shake the Northern lands, and during the Battle of Bravalla many warriors will cross the Rainbow Bridge and sit at Odin's right hand.

STARKAD AND THE DRAGONSLAYER

Beleaguered on all sides, King Hring fears for his kingdom. He resolves strike a blow that will resound throughout the Northlands and deter further raiders, and yet he must also defend his borders against the marauding Easterlings.

On the horns of a dilemma, he sends Starkad south to issue a challenge to the ruler of Burgundy, most far-famed of the kings of the Southlands: pay tribute or fight. The Burgundians choose war.

Yet in the coming fight, will Starkad at last meet his match?

STARKAD THE ACCURSED

Cursed by Thor, blessed by Odin, Starkad's three lifespans are near the end. Time for one last niddering deed--the murder of his own liege lord! Can Starkad hope to fulfil his deadly mission and escape vengeance?

Or does Valhalla await this grizzled old warrior?

Made in the USA
Coppell, TX
21 February 2022

73885760R00148